DANGER

The man came at Fargo, whipping the knife back and forth fiercely in the air. Fargo had no choice but to give ground. He couldn't go very far, though, because the edge of the dock was right behind him. He heard the other man floundering and slashing as he tried to climb out of the shallows and back onto the dock.

"You son of a bitch!" the knife wielder hissed at Fargo. He darted the blade at Fargo's eyes. Fargo jerked to the side, and as he did so, he stooped and drew his own knife from its sheath on his calf. The other man paused as Fargo came up with his Arkansas toothpick. Suddenly the narrow-bladed dirk he held in his hand didn't look nearly as dangerous. . . .

THE
TRAILSMAN
#254

NEBRASKA GUNRUNNERS

by

Jon Sharpe

Ø
A SIGNET BOOK

SIGNET
Published by New American Library, a division of
Penguin Putnam Inc., 375 Hudson Street,
New York, New York 10014, U.S.A.
Penguin Books Ltd, 80 Strand,
London WC2R 0RL, England
Penguin Books Australia Ltd, 250 Camberwell Road,
Camberwell, Victoria 3124, Australia
Penguin Books Canada Ltd, 10 Alcorn Avenue,
Toronto, Ontario, Canada M4V 3B2
Penguin Books (N.Z.) Ltd, 182–190 Wairau Road,
Auckland 10, New Zealand

Penguin Books Ltd, Registered Offices:
Harmondsworth, Middlesex, England

First published by Signet, an imprint of New American Library,
a division of Penguin Putnam Inc.

First Printing, December 2002
10 9 8 7 6 5 4 3 2 1

Copyright © Jon Sharpe, 2002
All rights reserved

The first chapter of this book previously appeared in *Dead Man's Hand,*
the two hundred fifty-third volume in this series.

REGISTERED TRADEMARK—MARCA REGISTRADA

Printed in the United States of America

The Trailsman

Beginnings . . . they bend the tree and mark the man. Skye Fargo was born when he was eighteen. Terror was his midwife, vengeance his first cry. Killing spawned Skye Fargo, ruthless, cold-blooded murder. Out of the acrid smoke of gunpowder still hanging in the air, he rose, cried out a promise never forgotten.

The Trailsman they began to call him all across the West: searcher, scout, hunter, the man who could see where others only looked, his skills for hire but not his soul, the man who lived each day to the fullest, yet trailed each tomorrow. Skye Fargo, the Trailsman, the seeker who could take the wildness of a land and the wanting of a woman and make them his own.

Nebraska Territory, 1860—
Where the plains run red with blood
and men seek their fortune in bullets

1

The Great Plains were not as flat and featureless as they might appear at first glance. Skye Fargo had ridden over them many times and knew them quite well. He knew the way the prairie rolled, rising to long, gentle crests, and then swooping down into shallow depressions, some natural and some of them wallows created by the vast herds of buffalo that roamed the landscape. Fargo knew as well how the terrain was scored and creased in places by creeks and dry washes. As he reined the Ovaro to a halt atop a small point of land and peered eastward with his lake-blue eyes, he knew that the seeming emptiness in front of him could contain all sorts of dangers for an unwary traveler. Indians had a habit of apparently appearing out of nowhere in these parts, and outlaws could be lurking in those gullies and washes, too. A pilgrim who was not careful was a pilgrim who might soon be dead.

Skye Fargo was no pilgrim. He was the Trailsman.

He nudged the black-and-white pinto forward into an easy lope that carried man and horse across the prairie at a ground-eating pace. The Platte River was off to Fargo's right, curving southeastward. Ahead of him, running down from the north, was the Elkhorn. Farther east lay the relatively new city of Omaha, which was just across the Missouri River from Council Bluffs, Iowa. For twenty years or so, Council Bluffs had been one of the jumping-off places for wagon trains full of immigrants bound for what they hoped would be paradise. When news of gold strikes in Colorado arrived, the city fathers of Council Bluffs had come up with the idea of establishing a new town on the western bank of the Missouri to better serve the thousands of new immigrants bound for the gold mines. In the half-dozen years since then, Council Bluffs had been far outstripped by Omaha as an outfitting point for wagon trains. Now the territorial capital of Nebraska, Omaha was quite a booming place.

Fargo had no doubt he would be able to find the things he was looking for there: a game of cards; a drink of whiskey; a real bed; and, most importantly, a warm, willing woman to share it with him.

He had spent the past month guiding an immigrant train as far as South Pass in Nebraska Territory, where the travelers had picked up another guide who would take them and their wagons on through the Rockies and over the Continental Divide. Fargo might have stayed with the wagon train the entire way, if a sudden fever had not claimed the lives of an entire family he had befriended. That cluster of lonely graves on the windswept prairie had reminded him too much of bitter losses in his own past, so when the train reached the trading post at South Pass, and he knew the pilgrims were in the capable hands of another guide, Fargo had turned and ridden away, heading east and keeping the mountains behind him.

By now the memories had receded, so he was looking forward with keen anticipation to spending some time in Omaha. As a rule, Fargo was not that fond of cities, but they came in mighty handy every so often, when a fella wanted to blow off some steam.

A few minutes later, Fargo tensed as the stallion slowed down and lifted its head, pricking up its ears. He was letting the Ovaro set the pace, as he usually did when there was no pressing need for speed. The horse's behavior told Fargo that it had seen or heard or smelled something out of the ordinary, or maybe a combination of all three things. Now that he had been alerted, he noticed that there was a distinct smell in the air, as if a cloud of dust had blown through here a short time earlier, and a faint haze lingered in the atmosphere.

That meant a large group of riders, Fargo thought. Out here on the plains, such a thing might be innocent . . . but the chances were greater that it boded ill for somebody.

The Ovaro did not stop, and Fargo did not rein in. He kept riding, seemingly unconcerned by anything around him, but his right hand went to the butt of the Colt on his hip and loosened the gun in its holster. His eyes flicked from side to side.

The stallion whinnied. With no more warning than that, a group of riders burst into view, urging their mounts up out of a wash to Fargo's right. He reined in sharply, pulling the big horse around in a half turn. His hand palmed out the Colt and started to lift it.

He stopped the gesture, not because he found himself facing the muzzles of half a dozen rifles but because he recognized the uniforms worn by the horsemen who were confronting him. The campaign caps and blue tunics and darker blue trousers with yellow stripes down the legs identified them as members of the United States Cavalry.

The men were all carrying .54 caliber carbines, which at the moment they had leveled at Fargo. "Hold it!" a strident voice shouted, and two more men rode out from behind the group of cavalrymen. One was a burly sergeant. The other bore the insignia of a lieutenant on his uniform. His face was young and untanned, Fargo noted, and that came as no surprise. There were plenty of shavetail lieutenants out here on the frontier. The army had a bad habit of sending its young, inexperienced officers West for some seasoning. All too often, instead of making wily veterans out of them as the brass intended, the frontier just made those shavetails dead.

"Mister, I'll give you three seconds to holster that gun!" the lieutenant yelled at Fargo. He started to count. "One! . . ."

With a wry quirk of his mouth, Fargo slid the heavy revolver back into its holster. He wasn't going to give this youngster an excuse to get trigger-happy. He didn't much care for his high-handed attitude, though.

"Don't get a burr under your saddle, Lieutenant," Fargo said, his deep, calm voice carrying over the prairie without the need for shouting. "I'm not looking for trouble."

The young officer spurred his horse closer. The sergeant stayed close by his side. Tall, with broad, heavy shoulders, the noncom looked like he had all the experience and seasoning that the lieutenant lacked.

The lieutenant reined in, facing Fargo from a distance of ten feet. "What are you doing out here, mister?" he demanded.

Fargo sat easy in the saddle, his hands now crossed and resting on the horn. "Didn't know the prairie was off-limits," he drawled, a faint, mocking smile on his lips.

"Just answer the lieutenant's question," the sergeant snapped. Fargo couldn't see any hair under the man's campaign cap. He appeared to be bald, despite being only in his thirties.

Fargo didn't like being bullied, and that seemed to be what these soldiers had in mind. But arguing with them would be just a waste of time, and besides, he tried to cooperate with the authorities, both military and civilian, whenever he could. "I'm bound for Omaha," he said. "Just looking to take it easy for a while and stock up on supplies while I'm there."

"Where are you coming from, and what were you doing there?" the lieutenant asked.

Fargo thought that the officer could have stood a lesson in frontier etiquette. It wasn't considered polite to ask a fella too many questions, especially when they concerned where he had been and what he was doing there. But again, Fargo wasn't looking to borrow trouble, so he said, "I've been guiding a wagon train to South Pass."

"Do you have any proof of that?"

The lieutenant's persistent suspicion was starting to raise Fargo's hackles a little. "I've still got some of the money those immigrants paid me," he said, "but one gold piece looks pretty much like another, I reckon."

"Watch that smart mouth, mister," the sergeant said as he glowered at Fargo.

"I can handle this, Sergeant Creed," the lieutenant snapped with a sidewise glare at the noncom. Fargo took note of that, too, as well as the narrow-eyed look that the sergeant gave his superior officer. There was no love lost between these two.

The lieutenant turned his attention back to Fargo and asked, "What's your name?"

That was about enough, Fargo decided. He said, "Why don't you tell me what this is all about, Lieutenant? Do you have a reason for all these questions—or do you just not have enough to do today?"

The lieutenant's mouth drew down into a thin, angry line. Fargo expected an angry outburst, but after a moment, the young man said, "I'm Lieutenant Jackson Ross, in command of this detail from Headquarters Company, Department of the Platte, in Omaha. We're searching for the men responsible for a crime."

"What sort of crime?"

"That's none of your concern."

"I think it is," Fargo said, "when a few minutes ago it sounded like you were practically accusing me of being mixed up in it."

With a visible effort, Lieutenant Ross controlled his temper and impatience. "Two days ago, a United States Army supply train was on its way through this area. It was attacked, and the supplies being carried on the wagons were stolen."

"What kind of supplies?"

"That really *is* none of your business," Ross said.

Fargo leaned forward a little in the saddle. "Let me think about this," he said. "Somebody jumps a bunch of army supply wagons and makes off with what they're carrying. I don't reckon anybody would go to that much trouble for some barrels of salt pork and beans. Sounds more like what they took must have been guns."

Sergeant Creed said, "If you're such a smart son of a bitch, maybe you can tell us where those rifles are now."

Lieutenant Ross shot him an angry glance, then said to Fargo, "It was a shipment of new rifles bound for Fort Laramie, if you must know. What can you tell us about the raid?"

Fargo shook his head. "Not a damned thing. Two days

ago I was a long way west of here. I haven't seen anybody suspicious between then and now, either. In fact, I haven't seen much of anybody. These plains are pretty empty between wagon trains."

"Why should we believe you?"

"Because I'm not in the habit of lying," Fargo said, his own irritation rising to the point where he was having trouble containing it.

"You'll pardon me, I'm sure, if I don't take your statements at face value."

Fargo said, "And you'll pardon me if I don't give a damn what you take and what you don't." He lifted the Ovaro's reins, preparing to ride around the cavalrymen. "Now, I'm going on my way."

Ross edged his horse over to block Fargo's path, and his hand moved to the snapped-down flap of the holster where he carried his sidearm. Creed said to him in a low, urgent voice, "Lieutenant, that fella can get his gun out and put four or five slugs through you by the time you unsnap that flap and haul out that pistol. Better take it easy."

Ross looked furious, but he took Creed's advice. He said contemptuously, "What would you have me do, then, Sergeant?"

"Leave this no-account drifter to me," Creed said, giving Fargo an ugly grin. "I'll beat the truth out of him."

Ross frowned. "I won't have you brawling with a civilian, Sergeant."

"What would you rather do with him? Have those troopers shoot him because he won't answer your questions?"

Ross hesitated before answering, torn by the situation in which his arrogance had placed him. Fargo could tell what the young officer was thinking. Ross didn't like the way Fargo had defied him, but it was an offense that hardly justified having the rest of the patrol open fire on him.

Coming to a decision, Ross said, "Very well, Sergeant. I'll leave the interrogation of this man to you."

That ugly grin stretched even farther across Creed's

face. "Thanks, Lieutenant. I won't let you down." He looked at Fargo. "All right, mister. Now it's just you and me."

Fargo made one last attempt to head off a situation he hadn't wanted to be involved in in the first place. "I'm telling you I don't know anything about any raid on a supply train."

Creed shook his head. "Too late. I don't believe you. Now you got to learn that you can't defy the U.S. Army."

Fargo supposed he could have told them who he was, explained that he had worked successfully with the army on many occasions, and dropped the names of quite a few well-known officers, up to and including a few generals, who could vouch for him.

But after the way Ross and Creed had acted, he just wasn't in the mood to be a peacemaker anymore.

Creed swung down from his mount and said, "Get off that fancy horse, mister." He took his pistol out of its holster and handed it to Ross, then removed his campaign cap and placed it on his saddle.

The lieutenant was starting to look worried, as if he wished he hadn't agreed to Creed's suggestion. He said, "Maybe this isn't such a good idea, Sergeant . . ."

"Don't you worry, sir," Creed said, his gaze intent on Fargo. "I'll find out what you want to know." He took a step closer to the Trailsman. "Are you gonna get down, or do I have to pull you out of that saddle?"

Fargo sighed, but he didn't really mind all that much what was about to happen. Maybe a good brawl would clear his head of the cobwebs that had been clogging it ever since he'd left the wagon train. He swung his right leg over the Ovaro's back and stepped down to the ground. He took off his gunbelt, looped it around the horn of his saddle, and placed his hat on top of it. He bent over and unstrapped the leather sheath that held the Arkansas toothpick on his right calf, slid the sheathed knife into the saddle boot with his Henry rifle. Then, unarmed, he turned to face Creed.

In what came as no surprise at all to Fargo, the burly

7

noncom was already lunging at him, fists balled and swinging.

Fargo ducked lithely to the left so that Creed's right fist swept harmlessly past his shoulder. He twisted and drove a punch into Creed's right side, hooking the blow. Creed grunted and jerked up the elbow closest to Fargo, aiming it at Fargo's face. The blow would have pulped Fargo's nose had it landed, but Fargo hunched his shoulder, lowered his head, and bore in, peppering Creed's midsection with short, hard punches. The flurry of blows made Creed stumble backward.

In trying to press his advantage, Fargo got too close. He realized that and tried to dart back, but he was too late. Creed caught his balance and with an angry yell threw himself forward, his arms going around Fargo in a bear hug. Fargo felt his booted feet come off the ground. He went over backward, landing in the dirt with stunning force. Creed's weight on top of him drove the air from his lungs and made him gasp for breath. The world turned red and black and spun crazily around Fargo for a second.

Knowing that he had to get Creed off of him, he brought up his knee, aiming the blow at the sergeant's groin. Creed twisted so that Fargo's knee hit him on the hip, but it was enough to topple him to the side. Fargo rolled in the other direction, came up on his hands and knees, and had time to gulp down one huge breath before he saw Creed coming at him. The sergeant's foot lashed out in a vicious kick aimed at Fargo's face.

Fargo got his hands up barely in time to catch Creed's boot and keep it from smashing into him. He heaved with all his might. Creed yelled and went over backward. Dust flew in the air as he landed on the ground. Now it was Fargo's turn. He leaped up and came down with both knees in Creed's belly. His fist sledged into Creed's jaw, bouncing the sergeant's bald head off the ground. One more blow would have stunned Creed and maybe ended the fight, but Creed got a leg up, hooked it around Fargo's throat, and levered him backward. Fargo went sprawling.

Creed must have engaged in hundreds of barracks brawls. He was an experienced, dangerous fighter. But Fargo had survived a rugged existence on the frontier, often being forced to fight for his life, and despite being a little smaller than Creed, he was almost as strong and definitely faster. He rolled over again, came up on his feet, and met Creed's bull-like charge with a solid left-right combination that rocked back the sergeant's head and brought him to an abrupt stop, as if he had run into a stone wall. Creed swung a couple of wild roundhouse punches. Fargo avoided them both and jabbed a blow to Creed's nose. Blood spurted as Creed howled in pain.

From that point on, for Fargo it was just a matter of picking his spots and doling out punishment. He snapped several more punches to Creed's bleeding nose, then switched his attention to the sergeant's mouth, jabbing at it until Creed's lips were as swollen and bloody as his nose. Creed kept throwing punches, but he had slowed down and Fargo had no trouble avoiding the blows. Fargo even had time to glance over at Lieutenant Ross and the other troopers. The men had been yelling encouragement to Creed at the beginning of the fight, but now they just stood there silently, with dumb, surprised looks on their faces. They probably weren't used to seeing Creed take a beating. Ross just sat on his horse and watched with a tight, angry look on his face. Neither he nor the soldiers tried to interfere, though.

Creed stumbled forward, swinging another wild punch. Fargo stepped inside it and launched an uppercut from his knees. His fist caught Creed under the jaw and drove the sergeant's head so far back that Fargo worried for a second that he had broken the larger man's neck. Creed's eyes rolled up in his head. As Fargo stepped back, Creed dropped to his knees, swayed back and forth for a second, and then pitched forward onto his face. His breathing made bubbling sounds as the air passed through his battered, blood-filled nose.

Fargo drew the back of his hand across his mouth, noting the smear of blood that the gesture left behind He had taken enough punches so that his lips were bleeding, too, though not nearly as much as Creed's were. He spat, then turned to the Ovaro and reached for his hat and gun.

"You're under arrest," Ross said, his voice shaking a little.

"Go to hell," Fargo said. He picked up his hat, put it on the back of his head, and started strapping the gunbelt around his lean hips.

"You assaulted a noncommissioned officer of the United States Army—"

"Creed threw the first punch. The whole thing was his idea in the first place."

"You refused to answer questions—"

"I don't like being treated like some sort of renegade," Fargo snapped. "My name is Skye Fargo. Why don't you go back to your headquarters in Omaha and ask your commanding officers if they think I had anything to do with ambushing that supply train? Better yet, send a message to Washington and ask General Winfield Scott the same question."

Ross's eyes widened at Fargo's mention of the commander of the entire army. "You know General Scott?"

"Old Fuss and Feathers? We've run into each other a time or two."

The lieutenant swallowed and said, "I . . . I'm not sure I ought to believe you . . ."

One of the troopers spoke up. "Lieutenant, beggin' your pardon, but if this fella is Skye Fargo, I reckon you can believe him, all right. I've heard that he's done quite a bit of scoutin' out here for us. He wouldn't go around stealin' rifles."

"Well, then . . ." Ross took a deep breath. "In that case, my apologies, Mr. Fargo. Surely, though, you can understand. The theft of those rifles is a serious crime, and my men and I have been charged with finding the culprits."

Fargo had a feeling that Ross would be lucky to find a snowflake in the middle of a blizzard, but he kept that thought to himself. Instead, he said, "I accept your apology, Lieutenant. And I'm sorry to hear about those stolen guns. But in the future, you need to keep a tighter rein on Sergeant Creed, no matter who you're looking for."

Ross's features stiffened. "I hardly think a civilian is in a position to give advice on military discipline and procedure."

Fargo strapped the Arkansas toothpick back on his leg. "I'm just saying, that's all." He took hold of the Ovaro's reins, grasped the saddlehorn, put a foot in the stirrup, and swung up on the stallion's back. "Like I said before, I'm headed for Omaha. If you have anything else you'd care to discuss, Lieutenant, you can look me up there."

He was about to ride away when a ragged voice rasped, "You . . . bastard."

Fargo looked around and saw that Creed had come to and pushed himself up on hands and knees. The sergeant's face was covered with blood as he stared up at Fargo, but the hatred he felt was clearly visible through that crimson mask.

"This ain't . . . over," Creed growled.

"As far as I'm concerned, it is," Fargo said.

Creed stood up, unsteady but on his feet again. "No, it ain't." His voice got a little stronger. "One o' these days, we'll finish it, you and me."

"Sergeant, that's enough," Ross said.

"No," Creed said. "Not hardly, it ain't."

Fargo wheeled the Ovaro and put it into a trot, but as he rode away, he could feel Creed's eyes boring holes in his back. He had made an enemy today, he told himself. A bad enemy. He would have to watch his back while he was in Omaha, just in case Creed tried to take his revenge while Fargo was there. He hoped it wouldn't come to that.

But if it did, the Trailsman would be ready . . . as always.

2

The unpleasant encounter with the cavalry slowed Fargo down enough so that night fell before he reached Omaha. He knew he had to be within a few miles of the city, though, so he pushed on despite the darkness. The surefooted Ovaro had no trouble negotiating the prairie, even at night. The stars overhead provided a considerable amount of light, and as the moon rose its silvery illumination washed over the landscape, making it almost as bright as day.

A short time later, he rode down a broad, dusty street between two rows of buildings. Covered boardwalks lined both sides of the street, fronting on the businesses. Fargo rode past general mercantiles, apothecaries, hardware stores, milliners, blacksmiths, livery stables, wagon yards, doctors' and lawyers' offices, several churches, a school, a gunsmith's shop, a saddlemaker's, and more than one saloon. Plenty of saloons, in fact. From the looks of it, there were more drinking and gambling and dancing establishments in Omaha than any other kind of enterprise—which made it just like most other towns on the frontier.

Fargo let his instincts guide him, and after a few minutes he reined the stallion to a halt in front of a saloon called the King's Crown. The place had a solid look about it. Not a hole-in-the-wall dive, but not as opulent as some of the other saloons in town. It seemed to be the sort of place where a man could get a decent drink, play a few hands of cards, and be comfortable while he was doing it.

That theory was put to the test a moment later as Fargo dismounted. He had just looped the Ovaro's reins over the hitch rail when a man came sailing through the batwinged entrance and came crashing into the street.

Another man came out onto the boardwalk and brushed his hands together in satisfaction as he looked down at the gent who had landed in the street. "And stay out!" the second man said. He was of medium height, Fargo judged, but the width of his shoulders and torso made him look shorter. He had thinning black hair and a heavy black mustache that curled up on the ends. The apron he wore over a homespun shirt marked him as either the bartender or owner of this saloon, quite possibly both.

The man looked over at Fargo, took in the buckskins, the broad-brimmed hat, the Colt with the well-worn grips resting easily in its holster, the heavy-bladed Arkansas toothpick in its fringed sheath. "Well," the man demanded, "are you as dangerous as you look, bucko?"

His accent was English, which helped explain the name of the saloon. Fargo had run into other Englishmen on the American frontier. It wasn't that uncommon an occurrence. But he hadn't encountered many who seemed as belligerent as this one. Today seemed to be his day for bumping into fellas who were on the prod.

"I'm not dangerous at all," he said in reply to the man's question. "I'm about as mild as a cottontail rabbit."

The Englishman snorted in derision. "I'll bet."

The man who had been thrown into the street struggled to his hands and knees. "Better watch out, mister!" he called to Fargo. "He's crazy!"

"Crazy, is it?" the Englishman said. He stepped down off the boardwalk and aimed a kick at the other man, who scrambled to his feet and dodged the blow. He broke into a run that carried him down the street. The Englishman balled his hands into fists, rested them on his hips, and said, "Good riddance."

"What did he do?" Fargo asked. "Cheat at cards? Try to rough up one of the girls?"

"Worse. He insulted the Queen."

Fargo tried not to grin. "I see."

"Said it was no wonder she was the virgin queen, since she looks like a sow. His words, not mine. Bloody barbarian."

Fargo inclined his head toward the batwings. "You run this place?"

"Indeed I do." The Englishman turned to face him more fully. "Gerald Lazenby, late of Her Majesty's Navy." He stuck out a hand.

Fargo took it and shook. "Skye Fargo," he introduced himself. "I was looking for a nice quiet place to have a drink, but it looks like I may have come to the wrong place."

"Nonsense! Come in, come in. This is the friendliest pub this side of London. You'll see." Lazenby put a companionable hand on Fargo's shoulder and steered him toward the entrance of the King's Crown.

Several men had come to the door to watch after Lazenby threw the man into the street. They backed off as Fargo and the proprietor came in. Lazenby went on, "You seem to be a man of breeding and taste, Mr. Fargo. The first drink is on the house."

"Mighty kind of you." Fargo stepped up to the bar while Lazenby went behind the hardwood. "Whiskey will do fine."

"All right." Lazenby reached for a bottle and glass, poured the drink for Fargo. "Interest you in something to eat?"

Fargo's stomach was growling a little. "I could do with some grub," he admitted. "Not kidney pie and blood pudding, though." He watched Lazenby to see if the comment was going to set off the saloonkeeper's fiery temper.

Lazenby just grinned. "Not to worry, mate. I know you American blokes. I'll have the cook fry you up a nice, thick steak."

"Now you're talking," Fargo said. He threw back the

14

drink, setting off a pleasant warmth in his belly, and found the whiskey potent and good. It was the real thing, not home-brewed panther piss.

Lazenby refilled the glass, and Fargo turned to rest an elbow on the bar as he sipped the whiskey and looked around the room. Things were settling down after the brief disturbance. Half a dozen men stood at the bar, and two dozen more sat at the tables scattered around the room. Some of them were drinking and playing cards; some were just drinking. Fargo saw only three women. None of them were young, but they were all reasonably attractive. Instead of the short, spangled getups saloon girls sometimes wore, they were dressed in long gowns with necklines low enough to show off their breasts. They delivered drinks to the tables and seemed to be skillfully avoiding sitting down at any of them. There was no piano player, but the talk and laughter and clink of poker chips and coins created a music of its own.

"What brings you to Omaha, Mr. Fargo?" Lazenby said. "If you don't mind my asking. I know some of you lads are a bit touchy about such things."

Fargo thought back to the afternoon and his run-in with the cavalry. He had been touchy about being questioned then, that was for sure. But Lazenby was being a lot friendlier with his inquiry than Lieutenant Ross and Sergeant Creed had been.

"I just felt like spending a little time in civilization," he said. "Been guiding a wagon train over to the Rockies for the past couple of months."

"Well, this is what passes for civilization in these parts, anyway," Lazenby said with a grin. "But for a man who's seen Trafalgar Square . . ."

Fargo took another sip of his drink. "How does a British sailor wind up in Nebraska Territory, anyway?"

"Ah, it's a long, sad story, a tale of woe and deceit—"

"And that's all the more reason not to bore this gentleman with it, Gerald," a new voice said. A woman's voice. Fargo turned to look at her, thinking that she must be light on her feet to be able to come up behind him that way without him hearing.

She was lovely; Fargo realized that on first sight. Dark red hair fell in thick ringlets around a fair-complexioned face lightly dusted with freckles. Large, intelligent green eyes looked squarely into his. She wore a high-necked, dark-green gown with white lace at the cuffs and bodice. Though modest in its cut, the dress was tight enough to reveal the sensuous curves of her body. The gaze she gave Fargo was cool but not unfriendly. He thought he detected interest in her eyes.

From behind the bar, Lazenby said, "Ah, Nora, you always ruin my stories—"

"Someone has to, Gerald." The redhead held out her hand to Fargo. "I'm Nora Lazenby."

Fargo took her hand, feeling the strength in her slender fingers. "The name's Skye Fargo. I'm pleased to meet you, Mrs. Lazenby."

"Mrs. Lazenby," she repeated, then laughed. "Please. It's Miss Lazenby. That great hulking brute is my brother, not my husband."

Fargo grinned. "In that case, I'm even more pleased to meet you, Miss Lazenby."

"Here, now!" Lazenby said. "If you have to flirt with the customers, Nora, couldn't you be a bit more discreet about it?"

"If I was discreet, it wouldn't be proper flirting, now would it?" Nora shot back at her brother.

Fargo suppressed a chuckle. Obviously, these two had a fondness for arguing with each other. He didn't want to get too involved with it, though, having seen how volatile Gerald Lazenby's temper was. Fargo wasn't afraid of the saloonkeeper, by any means, but he still had plenty of aches and pains from his scrap with Creed that afternoon. He didn't need to add any more bruises for a while yet.

Nora Lazenby turned her attention back to Fargo and said, "Mr. Fargo, would you care to have a seat at one of the tables with me? I can promise you a more stimulating conversation than anything you'd get from this lout of a brother of mine."

Fargo thought that just looking at her was stimulating

16

enough, but he kept that to himself. He said, "I'd be glad to join you."

Nora held out a hand across the bar. "Give me the bottle and another glass, Gerald."

"I won't," Lazenby declared.

She narrowed her eyes and turned them on him. "I own half of this place, or have you forgotten that?"

Grumbling, Lazenby handed over the bottle of whiskey and another glass. Nora held them both in one hand with practiced ease and linked her other arm with Fargo's to lead him across the room to an empty table.

When they were seated, Nora topped off Fargo's glass and poured a drink of her own. She held up the glass and said, "To new friends."

Fargo clinked his glass against hers. "I'll drink to that. A man can't have too many friends."

Nora sipped her whiskey and asked the same question her brother had. "What brings you to Omaha, Mr. Fargo?"

"Call me Skye," he suggested. "I've been out on the plains for a while. I wanted a few things that only a town can offer."

"Such as?"

Fargo shrugged. "Some good whiskey." He lifted the glass. "I've got that already. A game of cards. Something better to eat than jerky and hardtack. And a real bed." He left out the part about a woman to share the bed with him. If Nora Lazenby wanted to get around to that, it was up to her.

"I think we can provide you with all those things here at the King's Crown," she said. "Including the one you didn't mention."

Fargo raised his eyebrows. "Are you a mind reader, Miss Lazenby?"

"Nora," she said with a smile. "And with men, reading their minds isn't really that much of a challenge, now is it?"

Fargo just threw back the rest of his drink and grinned at her.

* * *

He wasn't disappointed when he saw her naked, later that night after he had walked her back to a small, neat house not far from the saloon.

She turned down the oil lamp on the small table beside the bed until a soft yellow glow filled the room where she had led him. Then she turned to face Fargo and started unbuttoning the dress she wore. Fargo let her undo a couple of the buttons, then he moved closer to her and murmured, "Let me help you with that."

His fingers deftly unfastened the buttons and spread the dress open, revealing the silk chemise beneath. He cupped her breasts through the silk and felt her nipples hardening against his palms. Her eyes were half closed and her lips were parted as she looked up at him. "You know how to treat a woman, don't you, Skye Fargo?" she whispered. "I could tell that you would, as soon as I saw you."

"I reckon a woman like you brings out the best in me," Fargo said. He lowered his head to kiss her, brushing his lips across hers lightly at first, then harder and with more urgency. She put her hands on his shoulders and squeezed.

After a moment, Fargo finished unbuttoning the dress and slipped it off of her. She stepped back, pushed down her petticoats, and grasped the hem of the chemise to pull it up and over her head. When she dropped it on the floor, she was naked except for her stockings. She didn't need a corset to give her such a sensuous shape. That was all natural. Her breasts were high and full and firm, slightly pear-shaped, with dark-pink nipples that jutted out proudly. The thatch of fine-spun hair at the juncture of her creamy thighs was dark red, just like the curls on her head.

"Now you," Nora said, moving closer to him again.

Fargo let her strip the buckskins off of him, once he had taken off his hat, gunbelt, and knife. She turned around and bent over to help him take off his boots, and that position gave him an enticing view of her finely rounded rump and the fleshy folds of her femininity just below it. He was tempted to reach out and run a finger along her opening to see if she was already wet, but he decided to wait. Sometimes it was good for a man to resist temptation, he told himself. Made it all the sweeter when he was finally rewarded.

When she had him nude, she pushed him back on the bed and knelt beside him. She licked her lips in anticipation, then lowered her head over his groin and took the head of his shaft into her mouth. She wrapped a hand around the rest of the thick pole of flesh and began pumping up and down with it. Fargo closed his eyes for a moment, relishing the sheer pleasure she was arousing in him.

He didn't want her to do all the work, though, so he reached over and grasped her hips, swung her around until she was straddling his head. He slipped a finger into her and felt the hot, wet sweetness of her core. Her hips undulated, making his finger slide in and out of her. They began to move even faster as he added another finger. Her mouth opened wider, took in more of his manhood.

Fargo used his thumbs to spread her open and began to lick her. She moaned around his shaft and thrust her body against his face. Fargo drove his tongue into her as far as he could and used his thumb to flick the little nubbin of flesh below her sweet mound. Her hips jerked, and she sucked even harder. Fargo knew he couldn't hold out much longer. She was going to drain him if she kept that up.

That was exactly what she wanted. She tore her lips away from his shaft long enough to gasp, "Yes, Skye, I want it this way! Give it to me now!"

Fargo always tried to oblige a lady. As Nora's mouth engulfed him again, he stopped holding back. He speared his tongue into her as his shaft throbbed powerfully and his climax took over.

With his heart pounding heavily in his chest, Fargo's head fell back against the pillow. He drew in several deep breaths as Nora sprawled atop him, equally winded. Her breasts were flattened against his belly, and he could feel her heart thumping. Her fingers caressed his thighs, digging into the hard muscles there. She turned her head, letting his softening shaft slip out of her mouth, and gasped, "Oh, my God, Skye, that was . . . that was magnificent!"

He couldn't have said it better himself. His hands rested on her back, massaging and caressing. "Yes, it was," he told her. "I'm mighty glad I decided to stop at the King's Crown."

Nora pushed herself up onto her elbows, then turned her head to look at him with a grin. "Not as glad as I am," she said.

She rolled off him and reversed herself so that they were lying in the same direction. Snuggling against his side, she went on, "You're going to stay here tonight, aren't you? There's so much we haven't done yet, so much I want to do."

"I'm not going anywhere," Fargo promised her. "Not unless that brother of yours busts in here with a scattergun and a preacher." He chuckled. "Then I'd be liable to go out that window."

"Skye!" Nora lifted her head to look down at him. "How can you say such a thing? You make it sound like some sort of . . . of badger game!"

"I'm sorry," Fargo said instantly, and he really was. "I didn't mean any offense, Nora. Gerald's just such a blustery sort of gent, it sounded like something he might do."

"Oh. Well, in that case, you're right. Gerald is quite the blusterer. But if he bursts in here with a preacher, *I'm* going out the window, too. I like my life. I have no desire to clutter it up with a husband just now."

Fargo tightened his arms around her. "Sounds like we think alike."

She reached down, cupped his organ, and stroked it gently but firmly. "Are we thinking the same thing right now?" she asked with a devilish smile. "Already?"

"I do believe I'm the one who read your mind this time," Fargo answered with a grin of his own as he rolled toward her, positioning himself over her now widespread legs. A second later he was inside her, and there was no doubt they were both riding the same thought.

3

Fargo slept late the next morning and woke up to the smell of food cooking. The aroma made him aware of just how hungry he was. Before leaving the King's Crown the night before, he'd had that steak Gerald Lazenby had promised him, but now he was ready for breakfast. He stretched, enjoying the feel of his bare skin against the sheets, and opened his eyes.

Sunlight slanted in through the gap in the curtains over the window, letting him know just how late it was. It had been months since he had slept until the sun was this high in the sky. And it felt good, too. Everybody needed a chance to relax every now and then, even the Trailsman.

Nora came in while he was getting dressed. She wore a blue robe, tightly belted around her trim waist, and her hair was still in a little disarray from sleep. Fargo thought she looked perfectly lovely.

"Good morning," she said, her voice as bright and cheerful as the sunlight coming in through the window. "I was beginning to think you were going to sleep the day away. I thought perhaps the smell of bangers would wake you up."

Fargo grinned. "Sausages, right?"

"Of course. You've had them before?"

"Once or twice. I've run into a few remittance men out here on the frontier."

"I see. You know that description doesn't apply to Gerald, don't you? We're not from a well-to-do family."

"I figured as much, when he said he'd been in the Royal Navy."

Wealthy British families had the habit of sending second sons—the ones who wouldn't inherit any of the family fortune—abroad so that they wouldn't be an embarrassment to their older brothers. As long as such men stayed out of England, they were sent money to live on: a remittance, thus the name. Some of them had come to America to make new lives for themselves here. Nothing unusual about that, Fargo reflected. Englishmen had been doing it ever since the *Mayflower* landed at Plymouth Rock.

"Gerald came here because of me," Nora went on. "My parents made the voyage to New York when I was quite young. It was that or go to debtors' prison for my father." A touch of bitterness crept into her voice. "Things weren't much easier on this side of The Pond. When both my father and my mother died, Gerald left the Navy and came to New York to fetch me. He decided that we would come West, though, instead of returning to England. I think he saw it as a new adventure. He's always been that sort, eager to go new places and see new things."

"I understand the feeling," Fargo said with a slight smile.

"At any rate, we wound up here in Omaha, and Gerald went to work in a saloon. It wasn't called the King's Crown then. He changed the name when he bought the place from the man who owned it."

"I thought you said the saloon was half yours."

"I had a bit of money I'd earned in New York." She didn't say how she had earned the money, and Fargo didn't ask. "It wasn't half, really, but Gerald insisted that we split ownership. He wouldn't have it any other way. He's full of bark and bluster, but he's really an old dear."

"I'm sure the fella he tossed out into the street last night feels the same way about him."

Nora laughed. "An old dear with a temper, I should say. Now come along, before breakfast gets cold."

Wearing his buckskins but not his boots, hat, or gunbelt, Fargo followed her into the kitchen and sat down at the table with her. Tendrils of steam rose from the cups of coffee next to their plates full of sausage, biscuits, and gravy. A pot of honey for the biscuits sat in the middle of the table. Fargo dug in, his appetite doing full justice to the food.

"Where's your brother this morning?" he asked between bites.

"Oh, Gerald stayed at the pub last night. Or rather, the saloon, I should say. I don't think I'll ever get used to not calling it a pub."

"He knew I'd be spending the night here?"

Nora shrugged prettily. "I didn't give him any sort of sign, if that's what you're asking, Skye. But Gerald has eyes. He could see that I like you."

"I'm grateful for his discretion, then."

She smiled across the top of her coffee cup at Fargo, her eyes twinkling. "So am I."

It would have been nice to take her back to bed after breakfast and make love to her again, but Fargo's curiosity about the theft of the army's rifles had been growing. He wanted to satisfy that itch first. Since Nora lived here in Omaha, where the army's departmental headquarters were located, she might have heard something about the incident. He wiped the last bit of gravy off his plate with a piece of biscuit, ate it, then asked, "Have you heard anything about some army supply wagons being ambushed lately?"

She frowned in surprise and said, "There was quite a bit of talk about it earlier in the week. I suppose the army would have preferred to keep it a secret, but the way people gossip, especially in saloons, that's impossible. We hear about almost everything that goes on in the entire territory."

"I thought that might be the case," Fargo said. "What can you tell me about it?"

"Why do you want to know? You're not some sort of lawman, are you, Skye?"

Fargo shook his head. "Nope. But I ran into an army patrol yesterday afternoon, and they were looking for the men responsible for stealing those rifles. At first they seemed to think I might have had something to do with it, just because I was riding across the prairie."

"That's ridiculous! Anyone could look at you and tell that you're not a thief."

Fargo grinned. "Not everybody is as perceptive as you are, I'm afraid. I've been taken for an owlhoot more than once by people who didn't know any better."

"Well, they were just foolish. You look like you can be dangerous when you need to be, but I can tell you're a decent man."

"I try," Fargo said. "What about the men who raided that supply train? I figure they weren't Indians."

Nora shook her head, but in this case, she was agreeing with him. "No, they weren't Indians. They were white. One of the soldiers who was wounded in the attack survived and managed to make it back here to Omaha before he died. He said the wagons had been ambushed by a large group of white men."

"He was the only survivor?" Fargo asked, his face and voice grim.

"And he died from his wounds a day later. Everyone else was killed at the scene."

Fargo looked down at the table and frowned. No wonder the patrol led by Lieutenant Jackson Ross had seemed so intent on their mission. The outlaws who had stolen the rifles had carried out an absolute massacre. Such wanton slaughter cried out for vengeance.

"Must have been a pretty big bunch of outlaws if they managed to wipe out an entire escort party like that."

"From what I've heard, they attacked at night," Nora said. "No one was expecting trouble."

"When exactly did this happen?"

"Four nights ago. Army patrols have spread out all over the territory since then, but as far as I know, they haven't found any sign of the thieves."

"There were no tracks to follow?"

Nora said, "Honestly, Skye, I don't know. You'd have to ask the army about that. You really are interested in this, aren't you?"

Fargo drained the last of the coffee from his cup. "I don't like murder, and from the sound of it, that's what this amounts to. And I know there's a good chance those rifles will wind up in the wrong hands. There's really nothing else the thieves can do with the guns except sell them to the Indians."

"And that will lead to more raids and more killing out on the prairie, won't it?"

Fargo nodded. "That's right."

"But you're not in the army, and you're not a lawman. You said so yourself. It's not up to you to do anything about this."

"Right again," Fargo admitted. That was true enough. He had come to Omaha to rest and relax, not to get mixed up in someone else's trouble. He would just have to keep reminding himself of that fact if he got the urge to do some investigating of his own.

"So what would you like to do today?" Nora asked him with a smile.

"I have a few ideas," Fargo said, smiling back at her.

Her fingers went to the belt of her dressing gown and untied it. "Do they involve going back to bed?" she asked as she slowly spread the gown open, revealing the valley between her breasts.

Fargo's smile widened into a grin. "There you go again," he said, "reading my mind."

After spending a pleasant morning in bed with Nora, Fargo got dressed again and walked down to the livery stable where he had left the Ovaro. He checked on the stallion, listened to the elderly hostler talk about what a fine-looking horse it was, and asked the old man about the ambush on the army supply wagon. The hostler had heard the same rumors as Nora and gave Fargo pretty much the same answers. Based on the testimony of the lone man who had made it back to Omaha before dying, it seemed pretty clear what had happened. The troops in the escort had been attacked in the middle of the night. The men on guard duty had been killed silently, probably with knives, and then the rest of the soldiers had been murdered in their sleep by a deadly volley of gunfire. The teamsters whose job it was to drive the wagons had been killed along with them. The lone survivor had lived through the raid because he was wounded and had passed out, and the killers had taken his unconsciousness for death. That had been pure carelessness on their part.

Without that twist of fate, it might have been days or even weeks before the outrage was discovered. The supply train wouldn't have been considered overdue at Fort Laramie for quite a while.

Fargo rubbed the Ovaro's muzzle, thanked the old man for the conversation, and started out into the street. The only plans he had were vague ones. He had promised Nora that he would eat supper with her at the King's Crown, but until then, he figured he would just look around the town.

He had gone only a few yards from the livery stable when a familiar voice said loudly, "There he is! There's the son of a bitch!"

Fargo stopped and turned to see Sergeant Creed stalking toward him from the opposite side of the street. Creed's face was bruised and swollen, and both eyes had black circles around them. Those eyes glittered with hate, and Creed's knobby-knuckled hands were clenched into fists at his sides.

Fargo hooked his thumbs in his belt, set his feet, and waited. He didn't want to have another brawl with Creed so soon, but if that was what the big noncom had in mind, Fargo would just have to oblige him. He wasn't going to let Creed take a swing at him without fighting back.

"Sergeant!" another voice barked. "Damn it, Sergeant Creed, *at ease*!"

The command rose into a bellow, and Creed came to a stop halfway across the street. He glared daggers at Fargo. His hatred was so intense it almost had a physical presence.

Fargo didn't pay much attention to Creed. He looked instead at the man who stalked past Creed and came toward him, followed by Lieutenant Ross. The newcomer wore the uniform of a colonel in the United States Army. He was tall and well-built, with a craggy, weathered face and crisp white hair under his black hat. A sheathed saber hung on his left hip, and he had a pair of gauntlets tucked behind his belt. He stopped a few feet away from Fargo and gave the Trailsman a curt nod.

"Mr. Fargo," he said as he extended a hand, "I'm Colonel Thomas Barrett. I've heard a great deal about you, and I'm pleased to make your acquaintance."

Fargo stepped forward to take Barrett's hand. "Colonel," he said with a nod. He looked past Barrett at Ross and Creed, then said, "If what you've heard about me came from the lieutenant and the sergeant here, I don't reckon much of it was good."

Barrett's bushy white brows drew down into a disapproving frown as he cast a glance over his shoulder at Ross and Creed. "When it comes to matters regarding the frontier, I'm not going to put too much stock in the opinions of men who don't recognize the name of Skye Fargo. I know several officers who have worked with you in the past and speak quite highly of you."

Fargo released Barrett's hand and said, "I'm glad to hear that."

"Mr. Fargo, would you be kind enough to accompany me back to departmental headquarters? There's an important matter I'd like to discuss with you, and I'd rather not do it in the middle of the street."

Fargo thought he had a pretty good idea what Barrett wanted to talk to him about. He knew as well what his answer would be to the question Barrett was likely to ask him. But he didn't want to discuss it in the street, either, so he nodded and said, "All right, Colonel."

Besides, Fargo thought, it was going to annoy the hell out of Creed if he cooperated and didn't give the sergeant any excuse to start more trouble.

Creed hung back as Fargo, Barrett, and Ross walked to the army headquarters compound on the edge of town. Barrett led the way into the commanding officer's office and motioned for Fargo to have a seat in front of the desk. Fargo did so while Barrett went behind the desk and Ross took another chair off to the side. Creed had stalked off elsewhere.

Barrett clasped his hands together on the desk and said, "Mr. Fargo, I won't waste your time. You know about the attack several nights ago that claimed the lives of more than two dozen of my men. You know as well that the killers made off with several hundred brand-new rifles being shipped to Fort Laramie. What I'd like to do is enlist your help in tracking down the men responsible for this outrage."

Fargo made a gesture with his hand intended to encompass the entire post around them. "You've got a garrison of troops at your disposal," he said to the colonel. "Why do you need me?"

Barrett shot a glance at Ross, then said, "Because those troops haven't been able to find a damned thing, and you're supposed to be one of the best this side of the Mississippi at reading sign and following a trail. They even call you the Trailsman, don't they?"

"Some do," Fargo allowed. "But from what I hear, the trail's four days cold. Chances are, I wouldn't be able to find anything, either."

"I can't believe that's true, after everything I've heard about you."

"Sometimes stories are exaggerated," Fargo said, his tone dry.

Barrett shook his head. "No, I'm convinced you're the man for the job."

Fargo glanced over at Ross and murmured, "That's funny. Yesterday the lieutenant seemed to be convinced I stole those rifles all by myself."

Ross's jaw clenched and his face turned a mottled red with suppressed anger. "If you want an apology for what happened, Mr. Fargo, I'll make one," he said. "Your own high-handed attitude contributed to the problem, however."

"Lieutenant, that'll be enough!" Barrett snapped. "And I happen to think that you and the sergeant *do* owe Mr. Fargo an apology. I know Luther Creed's a natural-born brawler, but there's no excuse for his behavior."

Fargo lifted a hand and shook his head. "That's all

right, Colonel," he said. "I reckon I was a mite prickly myself yesterday."

"Spare me your magnanimity," Ross muttered.

The lieutenant probably figured he didn't even know the meaning of a four-bit word like that, Fargo thought. He didn't make an issue of it, though. Instead he said to Barrett, "Colonel, I've had a hard couple of months. I didn't come to Omaha looking for a job, and I don't want to go to work for the army or for anybody else right now. Sorry."

"You want to let those murderers get away with what they've done?" Barrett demanded. "And you know their actions will lead to even more deaths once they sell those rifles to the hostiles."

Fargo grimaced. The colonel was making it hard for him to turn down the offer. During his years of wandering the frontier, Fargo had always tried to make the West a better place, a safer place for honest folks to live. If some Pawnee war chiefs, for example, got hold of those stolen rifles, they could wreak havoc from one end of the territory to the other. No farm, no isolated settlement, no wagon train rolling along the Oregon Trail would be safe, not to mention the more peaceful tribes whose natural order would be disturbed.

"Let me think about it, Colonel," Fargo said.

Barrett leaned forward. "There's no time to waste, Mr. Fargo. Like you said, the trail's four days cold already, and it's getting colder all the time."

"I also said let me think about it," Fargo said. He pushed himself to his feet. "I'll give my answer as soon as I can. That's the best I can do."

Barrett sighed. "Very well, then. I hope you come to the right conclusion."

"Whatever conclusion I come to, it'll be the right one for me." With that, Fargo turned and walked out of the colonel's office.

When he left the building, he found Sergeant Luther Creed lounging against one of the hitch rails just outside. Creed moved to get in his path, gave him an ugly grin, and asked, "Did the colonel hire you, Fargo?"

"He tried to," Fargo said. "I told him I'd have to think about it."

Creed spat on the ground. "We don't need no stinkin' civilian tellin' us what to do, not even the high-and-mighty Trailsman. You'd be better off keepin' your nose out of army business."

"I guess that's one of my failings," Fargo said. "I've never liked being told what was good for me."

"Does that mean you're takin' the colonel's offer?"

"It means I'm going to think about it, just like I told him. Now get the hell out of my way, Creed, or you and I will tangle again, right here and now."

Creed chuckled. "Maybe that's what I want."

"The colonel will throw you in the guardhouse if you start brawling again. Is *that* what you want?"

Creed's thick lips twisted in a snarl. "One of these days, Fargo," he said. "One of these days we'll settle this."

"Not today." Fargo stepped forward, his shoulder bumping Creed out of the way. Creed's fists bunched, but with a visible effort he stopped himself from taking a swing at Fargo. Fargo walked away, feeling Creed's eyes boring into his back with hatred.

That was getting to be an all too familiar sensation, Fargo thought. With all those emotions running rampant inside Creed, it probably wouldn't take long for the sergeant's anger to boil over.

When it did, Fargo would be ready.

4

Dusk was beginning to settle over Omaha. Fargo strolled down to the river and stood on the docks to look out over the broad, slow sweep of the Big Muddy. He thought about where the Missouri came from, about the Yellowstone, the Powder, the Milk, and all the other smaller rivers that flowed together to make up the Missouri, second only to the mighty Mississippi, which it joined with south of here at St. Louis. Fargo had ridden that country along the upper reaches of the Missouri more than once, seen the mountains and the plains, the wild places that called out to something deep inside him. He looked at the boats lined up along the docks, at the buildings that loomed and sprawled along the river, at the smoke that climbed into the sky from hundreds of chimneys, and he knew that the appeal of the city was fleeting for him. He had looked forward to reaching Omaha, but now, less than twenty-four hours after his arrival, he was ready to leave again, ready to ride out into the frontier that was his true home. He would miss Nora Lazenby; he had grown quite fond of her in a hurry. He would even miss her brother, who was likable despite his gruff exterior. But he wouldn't miss the city itself, not when the wilderness was beckoning to him.

That tipped the scales. It was one more reason—not that he really needed one—to accept Colonel Barrett's proposition and go after the marauders who had stolen those rifles. Besides, the threat the hijacked weapons posed was just too great. He couldn't turn his back on the inevitable spilled blood, not if there was a chance he could locate and recover the guns before they made their way into the hands of the Indians. And he knew there *was* a chance. A slim one maybe, but it existed nonetheless.

With that clear in his mind at last, Fargo turned away from the river—and right into trouble.

A stack of crates was nearby on the dock, having been unloaded there from a riverboat earlier in the day. Two men stepped out from behind the crates and blocked Fargo's path. In the gathering shadows, they were nothing but dark, man-sized shapes, patches of deeper darkness that moved toward Fargo.

He stopped in his tracks and listened to the echoes of his boots against the planks of the dock fading away. The two men didn't say anything. They just eased toward him in silence, moving apart a little so that he couldn't dart past them.

Fargo had been jumped before. He knew how these things went. He didn't waste any breath talking, either. If there was any chance these men could be talked out of what they had in mind for him, they wouldn't have followed him to the docks in the first place.

One man lifted his hand. He had a club of some sort in it. He made small circles in the air with the bludgeon, and Fargo heard him chuckle. The man was looking forward to what he thought was about to happen. The other man raised his hand, too, but instead of a club, the last fading light of day reflected off the blade of a knife. The man slid forward on the dock.

For a second, Fargo considered drawing his Colt and ventilating both of them. He knew he could gun them down before they could reach him. But in this poor light, he wouldn't be able to place his shots with any high degree of accuracy. He might wind up killing both of them, and he didn't want that.

He wanted to be able to question at least one of the men and find out who had sent them after him.

The one with the club rushed forward suddenly, sweeping a blow through the air at Fargo's head. Fargo ducked and let the club whistle harmlessly over his hat. He figured that the rush was more of a feint than anything else, and sure enough, the man with the knife darted toward him, the blade held low so that it could be brought up in a ripping, killing strike. Fargo was ready for it. The toe of his boot crashed against the wrist of the hand holding the knife. The man cried out in pain as Fargo's kick sent the blade spinning away. The knife landed in the river with a splash.

In dealing with the knife wielder, Fargo had to leave himself open for a backhanded blow from the club. He saw it coming from the corner of his eye, twisted his body, and took the stunning impact on his left shoulder. That arm went numb. Fargo staggered a couple of steps toward the edge of the dock, but he caught his balance before he fell off. The man with the club whipped the bludgeon at him again. Fargo jerked aside. The club swept down past him and hit the dock. The man grunted as the force of the blow shivered back up his arm.

Fargo stepped in quickly and jabbed a hard right into the man's face, rocking his head back. Fargo would have tried to follow up on his momentary advantage, but at that second, the other man tackled him from the side. He crashed into one of the pilings along the edge of the dock.

So far, the mostly silent fight had attracted no attention, despite the fact that several boats were tied up nearby and men were moving around on deck on the vessels. A dockside brawl was nothing unusual. Anybody who noticed the battle probably wouldn't summon the law. The rivermen appreciated a good knock-down-and-drag-out, though, and once they realized a fight was going on, they would flock to watch. The two men who had jumped Fargo wouldn't want that. They had followed him down here intending to kill him, and they wouldn't want any witnesses.

If he could hold them off for a few minutes longer, they would be forced to flee before the fracas attracted a crowd. Fargo didn't want that, either. If the two men escaped into the gathering darkness, he couldn't ask them any questions. He had to put a stop to this, and he had to do it now.

The man who had tackled him was trying to get his hands around Fargo's neck. Fargo drove an elbow into his face and knocked him backward. The one with the club rushed him again. Fargo's leg swept out, knocking the feet out from under the other man. With a startled, involuntary cry, he toppled right into the path of his companion. The man with the club tried to stop, but his momentum carried him forward. His feet tangled with the legs of the other man, and he fell.

Fargo was ready, swinging a punch that intersected perfectly with the jaw of the falling man. The blow twisted the man in midair. He dropped the club, and it clattered away as the man landed on the edge of the dock. His hands scrabbled at the rough planks, but he couldn't hold himself on. He rolled off, dropping the six or eight feet to the shallows at the edge of the river and landing with a huge splash in the Big Muddy.

Some of the feeling had come back into Fargo's left arm. He was able to reach down with both hands and grab the coat of the man who was still on the dock. As Fargo started to haul him upright, the man's hand lashed out, and Fargo saw at the last second that he had come up with another knife from somewhere, this one smaller but no less lethal. Fargo jerked back and shoved the man away at the same time. The tip of the blade caught him on the right forearm, drawing a line of fiery pain down his arm.

The man came at Fargo, whipping the knife back and forth fiercely in the air. Fargo had no choice but to give ground. He couldn't go very far, though, because the edge of the dock was right behind him. He heard the other man floundering and splashing as he tried to climb out of the shallows and back onto the dock.

"You son of a bitch!" the knife wielder hissed at Fargo. He darted the blade at Fargo's eyes. Fargo jerked to the side, and as he did so, he stooped and drew his own knife from its sheath on his calf. The other man paused as Fargo came up with the Arkansas toothpick.

Suddenly the narrow-bladed dirk he held in his hand didn't look nearly as dangerous.

Fargo knew the smaller blade was still deadly, though. It could kill a man just as dead as the heavier toothpick. He circled to his right, getting more room at his back. Water sloshed behind him. Fargo darted a glance over his shoulder and saw the other man pulling himself onto the dock. He was caught between them now.

The man with the knife must not have noticed that his companion was about to get back into the fray. And he must not have wanted to pit his dirk against Fargo's longer, heavier blade, because his arm suddenly jerked back and then flashed forward. Fargo saw the dirk flickering through the air toward him.

He dove forward. The dirk whispered past his ear and then struck something else with a solid thud. Fargo hit the dock and rolled over, and as he did so, he caught a glimpse of the second man. At just the wrong moment, the man had lunged to his feet with water streaming from his soaked clothes. The dirk had caught him in the chest, burying its keen, narrow blade in his heart. "No!" the man who had thrown the knife exclaimed in surprise.

The man with the knife in his chest stood there for a second. One hand came up and pawed feebly at the handle of the dirk. Then he fell forward, driving the blade even deeper into his chest when he hit the dock.

Fargo's roll had brought him up on one knee. From that position, he saw the other man break and run. Fargo could have thrown the Arkansas toothpick and brought him down; a bullet from the Colt would have been just as effective. But again, he couldn't guarantee that he wouldn't kill the man, and he didn't want that. He lunged to his feet and dashed off the dock, giving chase.

The man fled like a rat, scuttling through the darkening streets. Fargo's legs were longer, but his quarry had the speed of desperation. Fargo was able to keep him in sight for a couple of blocks as they raced past startled bystanders. Then the man darted into the black mouth of an alley and disappeared.

Fargo stopped at the alley, pressing his back against

the wall of one of the buildings. He stooped and slid his knife back in its sheath. As he straightened, he drew the Colt. He was going into that stygian passageway after the man he sought, but he wasn't going to do it without a gun in his hand.

He listened intently, but heard nothing coming from the alley, no rasp of breath, no scrape of boot leather on the ground. The fugitive was probably up there somewhere in the shadows doing the same thing he was, Fargo thought—listening as hard as possible.

With his customary silence and grace, the Trailsman moved into the alley, slipping along the wall of the building. He wanted to catch up to the would-be killer before the local sheriff or some of his deputies came along and spooked the man into running again. Fargo had some questions he wanted answered. Why had the two men tried to kill him? Who had sent them? Did this attempt on his life have anything to do with those stolen rifles? The idea seemed far-fetched, but why else would someone want him dead right now if not to stop him from joining the search for the thieves? The outlaws could have posted someone here in Omaha to keep an eye on things, and Fargo could have been recognized when he visited departmental headquarters with Colonel Barrett. From there it was an easy guess that the army was trying to enlist Fargo's help.

Those thoughts raced through Fargo's mind as he cat-footed along the alley. As far as he could tell, the theory made sense. He wanted to know who was working for the outlaws here in Omaha. If he could discover that, it would be the first step on a trail that might lead to the rest of the gang.

He held the Colt in front of him in his right hand. The fingers of his left hand brushed along the wall of the building, keeping him oriented in the thick darkness. Abruptly, that wall ran out and Fargo's fingers touched only empty air. That meant there was an alcove of some sort here, because he hadn't reached the far end of the alley. He could still see it several yards ahead of him, dimly outlined by the starlight that filtered down between the buildings.

Someone drew in a breath to his left. Fargo started to turn in that direction. Before he could do so, something crashed down across the wrist of his gun hand, knocking the revolver out of his grasp. He grunted as the pain from the blow shot up his arm.

Fargo ducked as something whistled through the air at his head. He didn't know what the man was using as a makeshift club—a barrel stave or something like that, more than likely—but he didn't want to find out. He lowered his shoulder and bulled forward into the alcove. The stink of fear sweat was sharp in his nose now. That would have given away the fugitive's presence, even if he hadn't jumped Fargo.

Fargo crashed into the man, and both of them fell to the hard-packed dirt floor of the alley. Both of Fargo's arms hurt from being walloped with clubs, but he managed to hook a pair of punches into the man's belly. Breath laden with the fumes of cheap whiskey gusted into Fargo's face. He threw another punch, felt it skid along the side of the man's head and rip part of his ear loose. The man yelled in agony.

He bucked his body upward, desperate to throw Fargo off of him. Fargo couldn't keep his balance and tumbled across the alley, losing his hat in the process. He sensed that his opponent would try to leap on top of him and got his hands up in time for his fingers to encounter the man's neck. Fargo grabbed on tight.

The man was smaller than Fargo, but he was wiry and frantic, a combination that allowed him to squirm part of the way loose and pepper a couple of blows into Fargo's face. The punches drove the back of Fargo's head against the hard ground. Fargo blacked out for a second, and that was long enough for the man to tear himself completely free. He scrambled to his feet and turned to run, tripped over something, and went sprawling. But when he came up again, he had Fargo's gun in his hands. Fargo's eyes had adjusted to the darkness by now, and he saw the muzzle of the Colt swinging toward him. His muscles tensed as he prepared to throw himself aside in an attempt to dodge a bullet.

Before Fargo could move, a gun blasted from the mouth of the alley and the flash from its muzzle lit up the darkness for a split second. In that instant of garish glare, Fargo saw the man who had been about to shoot him thrown forward by the slug that smashed into his back. The man landed on his face and skidded forward for a foot or so, then lay still.

No more shots were fired. Fargo glanced toward the mouth of the alley and saw a figure there ducking away. "Hey!" Fargo shouted, but the figure wasn't stopping. Fargo surged to his feet and ran along the alley. When he reached the end of it, he saw several people hurrying toward him, drawn by the sound of the shot, but no one was headed in the other direction. Whoever had fired that shot was already out of sight.

Fargo turned and stalked back to the man who lay motionless on the ground. Digging a lucifer out of the pocket of his buckskin shirt, Fargo snapped the match into life and narrowed his eyes against the harsh light that spilled from it. The glow from the burning match revealed a smallish man in patched range clothes. Fargo hunkered on his heels next to the man and used his free hand to search for a pulse in the man's neck. There wasn't one. He was dead.

Fargo's jaw tightened grimly. He had wanted to ask this man those questions, and now he would never get the chance to do that. Had that been the intention of the person who had shot him? Did Fargo's "rescuer" have some connection with the gang that had raided the army supply train, too?

Heavy footsteps sounded nearby. Fargo looked up, thinking he might be under attack again. His free hand started toward the Colt, which lay on the ground next to the man who had been killed.

A high-pitched voice said sharply, "Hold it, mister! Keep your paws away from that hogleg!"

Fargo pulled his hand back. "Are you the law?" he asked.

"That's right." A bulky shape loomed over him. "And I don't have to ask who you are."

"Oh?"

"You're the fella who just killed this gent," the man said with total conviction.

The lucifer had just about burned down to Fargo's fingers. He let go of it. The flame sizzled out as it hit the floor of the alley. "You've got that wrong, Sheriff," he said. "Somebody else shot this man."

"Is that so?" Another match rasped, and the flame was held to the wick of a bull's-eye lantern. As it caught, a broad circle of light filled the alley, revealing that several men had followed the sheriff. It was one of them who held the lantern. The sheriff himself was a thick-bodied, middle-aged man with graying curly hair behind a pushed-back hat, and a tin star pinned to his vest. He carried a shotgun in large, capable-looking hands. His voice might be boyish, but everything else about him said that he was a tough, seasoned, capable lawman. He went on, "Usually when I find a fella standing over a dead body, he's the one responsible."

"Not this time," Fargo insisted. He pointed. "Someone gunned him from the mouth of the alley, just before he could shoot me. You can see the bullet hit him in the back."

"What were the two of you doin' here in this alley, anyway?"

"I was trying to catch him, I'll admit that. He and a partner tried to kill me down on the docks a few minutes ago. The other man accidentally got a knife in the chest. This one threw it. I chased him up here."

"So you had something to do with that body on the dock!" the sheriff exclaimed. "I just come from there. You're just wreakin' havoc all over town tonight, ain't you, Mister . . . ?"

"Fargo. Skye Fargo."

The sheriff lifted his eyebrows. "The one they call the Trailsman?"

"That's right."

"Maybe you ain't lyin' after all." The lawman toed the

dead man onto his back, tucked the scattergun under his arm, and took the lantern from the man who had been holding it. Bending a little, the sheriff shone the light on the corpse. The dead man had a ratlike face with a bulbous nose that overhung a prominent mustache. A trickle of blood had leaked from the corner of his mouth. Fargo had never seen him before. The sheriff grunted and went on, "Typical hardcase. So's the one down on the dock, only considerable beefier than this one. They was probably tryin' to rob you."

"You think so?" Fargo said. He wasn't convinced of that.

"Yeah. I do my best to keep this a clean, law-abidin' town, but we got our share o' bad apples. This fella looks like he was one of the wormiest of the bunch."

Fargo couldn't argue with that. He said, "That's my gun he was about to use on me. You mind if I pick it up now?"

"Nah, I reckon not. Colonel Barrett told me about you, Fargo, and I heard plenty o' stories myself. I 'spose I can trust you." The sheriff put out a hand. "I'm Ed Madison."

"I'd say I'm pleased to meet you, Sheriff," Fargo said as he shook hands with Madison, "but under the circumstances . . ." He inclined his head toward the corpse at their feet.

Madison gave a grim chuckle. "I know what you mean. Come on back to the office with me, and we'll palaver a while about this." To the men with him, he added, "Some o' you boys haul this gent down to the undertaker's. Reckon the other one's already there by now."

Fargo knew that Nora Lazenby was waiting to have supper with him by this time, but he didn't argue with the sheriff. He liked to cooperate with the authorities whenever he could. He just hoped Nora would be patient.

"Hold on a minute," Madison said as several of the men got hold of the corpse and started to lift it. Madison leaned closer and shone the light in the dead man's face again. "There's somethin' familiar about this cuss. I've seen him somewhere before, if I could just recollect where . . ." Suddenly Madison lifted his head, shot a sharp glance at Fargo. "Damn, I know where this hombre comes from, him and the other one both. It just took me a minute to place 'em."

"If you know, Sheriff, I'd appreciate it if you'd tell me," Fargo said.

"Sure. Both of those boys are from Helldorado."

5

"El Dorado?" Fargo said a few minutes later when he and Sheriff Ed Madison were both seated in Madison's office.

"Nope. *Hell*dorado. And believe you me, the name fits. If there's a pure-dee hellhole anywhere in Nebraska Territory, that's the place."

Fargo thumbed his hat back. "I thought I knew most of the settlements around here."

"It ain't been around that long. Place sprung up about a year ago. It's three days' ride west of here, on the south bank of the Platte. My jurisdiction don't extend that far, but I rode over there anyway a couple of months ago, tryin' to get a line on some fellas who stole some horses and headed in that direction. That's when I saw those two who wound up dead tonight."

"You recall where in Helldorado you saw them?" Fargo asked.

"In one of the saloons." Madison tipped back his chair and rocked a little on it, his bulk making the rear legs groan as they supported his weight. "To tell you the truth, Mr. Fargo, I didn't hang around there for very long. I got the feelin' it ain't a place that's very friendly to the law, if you know what I mean."

Fargo nodded. He had seen other settlements like that, wide open and not wanting anyone from outside to interfere with what went on there. They were popular with outlaws. Men who were on the dodge could stop there, spend some of the loot from their crimes on whiskey and women, and stock up on supplies. All the citizens of such towns weren't necessarily criminals themselves, but they usually turned a blind eye to the depredations of the owlhoots who were passing through.

"Who does have jurisdiction over the area?" Fargo asked.

"Well, now, those parts are unincorporated, so there ain't no sheriff. Maybe a local marshal, but that'd be all. I guess the army could go in and take charge if they wanted to put the town under martial law."

"Why hasn't Colonel Barrett done that? It seems to me that would be the most likely place to start looking for the men who raided those supply wagons and stole those guns."

Madison nodded. "Yep, that makes sense, all right. And I think the colonel sent a patrol over there to poke around. But the folks who live in Helldorado just said they didn't know nothin' about it, and the army couldn't prove otherwise. That left the colonel up a creek."

Fargo frowned. He was beginning to understand why Colonel Barrett had been so eager to enlist his help. Fargo was a civilian; he didn't have to operate according to all the rules and regulations that the army did. He could go into Helldorado and stir up a hornet's nest without having to worry about the reaction of the War Department in Washington.

Madison leaned forward in his cracked leather chair. "You reckon those boys who jumped you tonight got somethin' to do with them stolen rifles?"

"I thought you said they were probably just trying to rob me," Fargo pointed out.

"That was before I remembered seein' 'em in Helldorado. And before I put it all together with what the colonel told me about how he'd talked to you earlier today."

Fargo smiled faintly. "It sounds almost like you and Barrett came up with all this in order to get me to take the job."

"How in blazes would we do that?" Madison demanded, his face flushing with anger. "We sure as hell didn't send those two hardcases after you!"

"Take it easy, Sheriff," Fargo said. "I know you didn't have anything to do with them trying to kill me. But you can't deny that it worked out well for you and Barrett."

"You mean you're goin' to Helldorado to get to the bottom of this?"

Fargo pushed himself to his feet. "You can tell the colonel as much when you see him. The way I figure, just because those two failed doesn't mean that whoever sent them after me will give up. Somebody considers me enough of a threat to want me dead." He smiled again. "So I reckon I might as well be one."

Nora looked up from the table in the King's Crown as Fargo approached a short time later. Her green eyes snapped with anger. "I expected you quite a while ago, Skye," she said as he pulled back a chair.

"Sorry. I was a mite busy."

"Doing what?"

"Keeping a couple of owlhoots from killing me."

The anger in Nora's eyes went away. Instead, they widened in surprise. "Killing you?" she repeated. She reached across the table and clasped one of his hands. "My God, Skye, what happened?"

"You haven't heard?"

"I heard a couple of men talking about some sort of ruckus down on the docks . . . Was that you? I heard that a man was stabbed to death, and another one shot!"

Fargo nodded. "That's about the size of it."

"You killed them?"

"As a matter of fact, no. Not either one of them. But I was there when both of them died."

He had been thinking about the mysterious figure that had gunned down the man in the alley. The more he considered it, the more likely it seemed that the killer had acted to prevent the man from talking. A dead man couldn't confess to anything or implicate anyone else.

And yet there was still a shred of doubt in Fargo's mind. The man had been about to shoot *him*, after all. Maybe the unknown gunman had acted to save Fargo's life. Maybe he was just a Good Samaritan who had come along in time to see a cold-blooded killing about to take place and had acted to stop it. Such a person might not want to get involved with the law. Fargo had to admit it was possible. To reach any definite conclusions, he had to have more to go on.

"This is terrible," Nora said. "I'm sorry, Skye. You come in here having barely escaped with your life, and I start acting like some sort of jealous shrew . . ."

"It's all right," Fargo assured her. "A woman as pretty as you shouldn't ever be disappointed. It'd take a matter of life and death to make a man miss having dinner with you."

Nora looked at him for a second, then laughed. "All right, don't overdo the gallantry. I know you're having a bit of sport with me—"

"Not at all," Fargo said with a grin.

"And I promise not to sound so much like a wife in the future," Nora went on. She signaled to her brother behind the bar. "I'll have our supper brought out now."

Fargo nodded. "Sounds good."

The food *was* good, but Fargo didn't really pay much attention to it. His mind was on everything that had happened and the job that he had facing him. Not only that, but also the aches and pains of two major brawls in two days were beginning to take a toll on him. A part of him wanted to just crawl into bed and sleep for ten or twelve hours.

Another part wanted to crawl into bed with Nora Lazenby and *not* sleep for a good long while. He would be leaving for Helldorado in the morning; he had decided that already. So he wanted to have a proper farewell with Nora tonight.

"You seem awfully distracted, Skye," she said as they were finishing their meal with bowls of deep-dish apple pie.

"I've got some things on my mind, all right," he admitted.

"Sometimes you think too much." She took his hand again, and the warmth of her fingers felt good to Fargo. "You should let yourself relax and enjoy life."

He grinned across the table at her. "I reckon I enjoy life more than most folks."

"Prove it. Come back to my house and make love to me."

That was the sort of challenge Fargo liked.

He draped Nora's shawl around her shoulders as she stood up, then linked arms with her and led her out of the saloon. Gerald Lazenby watched them go. He had a grin on his face, as if he knew what his sister was up to and completely approved. Well, at least Lazenby wasn't the overprotective sort, Fargo thought.

The night air had a touch of coolness to it that Fargo enjoyed. As he and Nora walked toward the house, he pondered when he ought to tell her that he would be riding out in the morning. He didn't want to ruin what was going to happen between them tonight, but on the other hand, he didn't like lying, even by omission. The only fair thing, he decided, was to be truthful with her.

"I'm going to see if I can find any trace of the outlaws who stole those army rifles," he said. "I think the men who jumped me tonight might have some connection with the gang."

Nora didn't break stride as she walked beside him, but he felt the muscles in her arm tense a little. "That means you'll be leaving?" she asked.

"First thing in the morning."

"That's a shame. I so enjoyed the way you slept late this morning . . . and what happened after you woke up."

"I enjoyed it, too," Fargo said.

She squeezed his arm. "I know."

They walked on in silence for a few moments. Fargo's eyes were in constant motion and his other senses were alert as well, searching for any sign of trouble. Just because the first attempt on his life had been a failure didn't mean the people who wanted him dead wouldn't try again, maybe as soon as this very night. He probably shouldn't have left the saloon with Nora, he reflected. He might be putting her life in danger just by being with her.

"Well, if you're leaving in the morning, we'll just have to make the most of tonight," she finally said.

Fargo smiled. "I was hoping that was the way you'd feel about it."

"I'm disappointed, mind you. Any girl would be once she'd got to know you, Skye Fargo. But I guess you pleased the colonel."

"I don't reckon I care whether he was pleased or not," Fargo said. "The only one I'm interested in pleasing tonight is you."

A short time later, that was exactly what he was doing. Nora had poured a drink of brandy for Fargo, then disappeared into her bedroom with instructions for him to wait where he was. When she reappeared a few minutes later, she was a lovely vision in a sheer, pale-green gown that revealed more of her beautiful body than it concealed. Fargo drained the rest of the brandy from the snifter, set it aside, and opened his arms as Nora came toward him. She lifted her head to receive his kiss. Their mouths melded together as Fargo put his arms around her. His hands slid down her back to cup her bottom and press her pelvis against him. Her tongue slid into his mouth as his erect shaft prodded the softness of her abdomen.

When they broke the kiss a few moments later, Fargo said, "You're one of the loveliest women I've ever seen, Nora."

"You're quite the flatterer, Skye." She rested a hand against his jaw with its close-cropped dark beard.

"No flattery, just fact," he said with a smile.

"And you've known a great many women, I suppose."

"A few," he allowed.

Nora laughed. "More than a few, I'd say. I can't imagine any woman with an ounce of life and passion in her not wanting you as soon as she laid eyes on you."

"Believe it or not, some of them seem to be immune to my charms."

"Maybe they'd like to think so, and perhaps they even

act like it, but deep down . . ." She shook her head. "No, Skye. They want you as much as I do."

"But tonight, I'm here with you."

"I know. So I have to take advantage of that fact . . ." Nora's hand moved between them and caressed his manhood through the buckskin trousers. "You have entirely too many clothes on, sir."

"We'll just have to do something about that," Fargo said.

Moments later, they were in her bed. Between the two of them, they had stripped off all of Fargo's clothes, but Nora still wore the light-green gown. He lay on his back while she sat beside him, her hands toying with the long, thick pole that jutted up proudly from his groin. While she fondled him, he filled a hand with the nearer of her breasts, cupping the creamy globe in his palm. His thumb found the hard bud of her nipple and strummed it lightly. She sighed in pleasure and tightened her fingers around his shaft.

"I want to ride you, Skye," Nora said. "I know it's shameless of me, but I want to feel you deep inside me."

"It's not shameless at all," he told her. "Wanting another person is about as pure an emotion as you can find."

She lifted the gown and swung her leg over his hips, straddling him. With her right hand, she reached behind her to grasp his shaft and guide it into her as she lowered herself onto him. He felt the wet heat of her core as it met the head of his organ, and then that heat slickly engulfed him. The urge was to thrust into her and fill her right away, but Fargo held back and allowed her to set the pace. She descended slowly, taking him in little by little. It was maddening, but it was also incredibly exciting.

When he was finally sheathed completely within her, she leaned back slightly and rocked her hips from side to side as she smiled down at him in the soft glow of the lamp on the table beside the bed. "My, that feels so good," she said in a throaty half-whisper.

Fargo groaned in agreement. He rested his hands on her widespread legs and pressed his thumbs into the muscles of her inner thighs. Her hips pumped in reaction to his touch.

Nora grasped the hem of her gown and peeled it up and over her head, then tossed it aside so that she was gloriously nude as she rode him. He raised his hands from her thighs to her breasts and cupped both of them, kneading and squeezing them and stroking the erect nipples. Nora began to pant in arousal as her hips moved faster. Fargo continued to let her set the pace and the tone of their lovemaking. She leaned forward, her face soft with desire and her eyes heavy-lidded, and with her hands resting on his chest to brace her, she began to thrust her hips back and forth fast and hard. She caught her bottom lip between her even white teeth.

Suddenly she cried out, unable to restrain herself any longer. She drove her hips down at him, and the buttery walls of her sex clasped him, spasming around his shaft. She threw her head back and closed her eyes as waves of pleasure crashed over her.

After a long moment, her head lolled forward again, and she let herself sprawl on Fargo's broad, muscular chest. She kissed his shoulder, his throat, his jaw, his chin, and finally his mouth. Fargo put a hand behind her head, running his fingers through her thick red hair, and held her there as his tongue caressed her lips and then slid forward to explore the warm, wet cavern of her mouth. Nora began to make a sound of satisfaction deep in her chest as she sucked on his tongue. Her breasts were flattened against Fargo's chest, and he could feel her heart beating a mile a minute.

She was too breathless to continue the kiss for long. She lifted her head, gazed down into his eyes, and said, "Skye . . . that was . . . unbelievable."

"Believe it," Fargo told her. "And believe me when I say it's going to get even better."

"I don't see how it could!"

Fargo grinned and whispered something in her ear.

She looked down at him, wide-eyed in amazement. "You didn't?" she exclaimed. "I never noticed . . . I was so excited myself . . . you're sure?"

Fargo's shaft was still rock-hard and throbbing with passion. "I'm sure," he told her as he grasped her hips, steadied her, and began to thrust powerfully in and out of her.

"Oh, my God!" Nora practically howled as Fargo drove into her. He tipped his hips up from the bed and reached even greater depths than before. Her core was drenched with the juices of her passion. Fargo reveled in the delicious heat and wetness of her, and he felt his own culmination stampeding toward him. He thrust up as Nora slammed her pelvis down, and that was the instant at which he began to erupt. Spasm after spasm shook him as he emptied himself inside of her. Though Nora had had a climax of her own only minutes earlier, another one washed through her as she collapsed into his arms.

Like all good things, it had to come to an end. They held each other tightly as they caught their breath and their galloping pulses slowed. Fargo stroked her red hair and kissed her forehead.

He would be riding out in the morning into unknown dangers but he knew that no matter what happened he was better off now than he was before. No matter that he had known her for only two nights, considering what his state of mind was when he had arrived in town—being with Nora had made all the difference.

Two nights with Nora. Fargo smiled. He liked the sound of that. It was going to make a good memory, one of many for the Trailsman.

Fluffy white clouds floated in the blue sky overhead as Fargo rode west. The stallion's ground-eating gait soon left Omaha far behind. When Fargo glanced back, he could see no sign of the city except a faint haze in the sky from its chimneys. After a few more miles, even that was gone.

Not that there were no signs of civilization out here

on the prairie. Fargo passed an occasional sod hut where a farmer had homesteaded instead of immigrating farther west. The soil here was good, and Fargo could foresee a day when all this land was covered with farms. That wouldn't happen for a while yet, though, and he was glad of that. The wild places seemed to shrink a little more with the passing of every year. Most folks regarded that as a good thing. Fargo wasn't so sure. Just because something was inevitable didn't mean it was necessarily the best for everybody.

6

Fargo stopped at midday and let the Ovaro graze while he made a meal of some jerky and hardtack he'd brought from Omaha. After washing down the food with water from his canteen, he looked toward the East, checking his back trail. He didn't really expect to see anything—if anybody was following him, they would probably take pains not to be seen—but he was surprised when he noticed a tiny black dot far behind him. He caught only a brief glimpse, but it was enough for him to recognize the shape as a rider. More than likely, he never would have seen whoever it was if they hadn't topped one of the small, rolling hills at just the right instant to be highlighted by the sun from Fargo's point of view.

Fargo ran a thumbnail along his jawline and frowned in thought. Just because someone was a mile or more back there, heading in the same direction he was, that didn't mean the rider was necessarily following him. It was possible the person had business of their own out here and had no connection with him whatsoever. Sure, that was possible, Fargo thought.

But he didn't believe it for a second.

He didn't delay for long. Soon, he was pushing on again, and he rode steadily all through the afternoon, stopping to make camp only when dusk began dropping down over the prairie. He didn't light a fire, preferring to make a cold camp even though there were plenty of buffalo chips around that he could have burned. Bands of Pawnee and Arapaho renegades sometimes roamed this far east, and it wasn't unheard of for a Sioux war party to drift this far south. Fargo didn't mind doing without the comfort of a fire if it meant he was more likely to keep his hair.

Whoever was behind him wasn't so cautious. As Fargo sat cross-legged on the ground and gnawed a strip of jerked meat, he looked to the East and saw a tiny pinprick of light. The campfire was a small one, but out here on this mostly flat prairie, any light could be seen for a long way. Fargo had pushed the Ovaro fairly hard during the afternoon, and the person following him had lost some ground. He estimated that the campfire was more than a mile and a half away.

If he was being followed, it might not be for long. Not if the follower was careless enough to announce his presence so openly. On the frontier, bad things tended to happen to people who were that foolish.

Knowing that the stallion would alert him if anybody came too close, Fargo rolled in his blankets and went to sleep. His last thoughts before he dozed off were of Nora Lazenby. He wondered what she was doing tonight, and he hoped that she was happy.

Two days of hard riding had done little to sap the big stallion's strength. Fargo was able to maintain a fast pace. By late afternoon, he thought he ought to be getting close to Helldorado. He had been following the Platte River ever since leaving Omaha, and since the settlement was supposed to be located on the south bank of the Platte, he knew he hadn't missed it. His keen eyes searched the horizon and discovered a few tendrils of smoke rising into the sky. That was it, Fargo thought. He had come to Helldorado.

A short time later, the buildings of the settlement came into view. The main street ran north and south, perpendicular to the Platte. Helldorado was a lot smaller than Omaha. Its business district comprised three blocks, and a dozen or so houses and cabins were clustered at the lower end of town around a single cross street. To the north was the wide, shallow river, which broke into several different channels separated by strips of marshy, treacherous ground that were more water than dirt.

Fargo rode to the northern end of the street and turned to his left, reining in the stallion to take a look at the town. Most of the businesses seemed to be saloons, though he saw a couple of general stores, a blacksmith shop, and a livery stable. There were no churches and no school. That came as no surprise to Fargo. From what he had heard of Helldorado, the people who lived here would have little interest in either education or soul-saving.

Heeling the stallion into a walk, Fargo rode slowly down the street. Quite a few people were on the board-walks in front of the saloons, and all of them were men. No women were in sight anywhere. Several of the men glanced suspiciously in Fargo's direction, while others watched him with open curiosity. He headed for the largest building in town, the only one that had an actual second story, as opposed to the false fronts on several other structures. Out here on the treeless prairie, it must have cost quite a bit to freight in the lumber to construct the building. A large sign across the front was embla-zoned with the simple legend Bates Saloon. Fargo reined to a halt in front of the place, dismounted, and looped the Ovaro's reins over one of the several hitch rails be-side the boardwalk.

Several men were sitting in ladder-back chairs along the boardwalk in front of the saloon. All of them were dressed in rough range clothes and had gunbelts strapped around their waists. One of them looked at Fargo with a particular intensity. He was lean almost to the point of scrawniness and had a hatchet face in which his dark eyes burned with banked fires. A flat-crowned black hat sat squarely on his head, and he wore a black vest over a shirt that had once been white but was now more of a dirty gray. Black whipcord pants and black stovepipe boots completed the man's outfit. He was even more gun-hung than the other men, with a pair of crossed car-tridge belts around his skinny hips and a black-butted Colt holstered on each side. Fargo knew the man's get-up was intended to make him look dangerous, but to Fargo's eyes it seemed vaguely ridiculous. None of that mattered, though, if the gunman possessed sufficient speed with those sinister-looking revolvers. Even a show-off could be deadly if he was fast enough with his guns.

The man had his chair leaned back. One foot was propped on the boardwalk's railing to keep him balanced. He put his foot down and let the front legs of the chair thump onto the planks as he leaned forward. At the same time, Fargo came up the two steps onto the boardwalk.

"Hey!" the hatchet-faced man said sharply. "Where do you think you're goin'?"

Fargo used his left hand to point at the batwinged entrance of the saloon. "Going inside to get a drink," he said in a deceptively mild voice. "It's been a long ride."

Hatchet-face came to his feet. "Yeah? Where'd you come from?"

That was considered an impolite question on the frontier, but Fargo didn't show any offense. "Omaha," he said.

Hatchet-face spat on the boardwalk, coming close to Fargo's foot with the gob of spittle. "Omaha!" he repeated. "I hate that place."

"I didn't much care for it myself," Fargo said.

He knew perfectly well what the hatchet-faced gunman was doing. The man wanted to prod him into a fight. He had never seen Fargo until a couple of minutes ago, but that didn't matter. He was bored, looking for trouble, looking for somebody to kill. The need to spill blood was visible in the man's dark eyes. Fargo looked like the sort of man who could put up a fight and provide an interesting challenge, but clearly the gunman didn't consider him a real threat.

Hatchet-face thrust out his blade of a jaw and said belligerently, "Well, I don't care for you, mister. What do you have to say about that?"

"I say it's a free country, friend," Fargo said as he reached up with his left hand and rested it on one of the batwings.

The gunman grabbed the door. "I didn't say you could go in there!"

"I didn't ask your permission," Fargo said.

"You son of a bitch!" The man let go of the door and his hands darted toward his guns as he crowded toward Fargo. "Don't you draw on me!"

Fargo knew exactly what the gunman was doing. By shouting out that warning, he was setting up a situation in which he could claim that Fargo had gone for his gun first, making the killing a case of self-defense. Fargo wasn't sure why he bothered; according to Sheriff Madison in Omaha, there was no law in Helldorado to worry about. Habit, maybe, from all the other cold-blooded killings Hatchet-face had carried out.

Fargo didn't care, and he didn't fall into the trap. Instead of reaching for his Colt, he slammed the batwing door he was holding into the gunman's belly and sternum. That knocked the man back a step and gave Fargo room to throw a punch with his other hand. His fist crashed into the man's lantern jaw and slewed his head around. He had his hands on the butts of his guns, but he was too stunned to pull them from their holsters. Fargo hit him again, with a left this time. The blow sent the man stumbling against the wall. Fargo kicked his feet out from under him.

The man sprawled on the boardwalk. His guns fell out of their holsters and slid along the planks. Hatchet-face reached a long-fingered hand toward one of them.

The sound of the hammer on Fargo's Colt being eared back made him stop in mid-reach. He glanced up, and the muzzle of the revolver must have looked at least twice as big around to him as it really was.

"I wouldn't if I were you," Fargo said.

Breath rasped in the man's throat. Fargo could tell that he wanted desperately to grab that pistol and blaze away with it, but he w~~ ld never have the chance to do that. Fargo could put ~ullet through his brain as soon as his fingers touched the gun. With a muttered curse, the man drew his hand away.

"That's being smart," Fargo said. He glanced around.

The other men on the boardwalk were watching him intently. Some of them looked angry, and he supposed those were Hatchet-face's friends. Others were expressionless, but Fargo thought he detected amusement lurking in their eyes. A man as arrogant as Hatchet-face seemed to be, probably tried to lord it over everybody around him, and he likely made life miserable for a lot of folks. Some of them probably liked seeing him taken down a peg.

"Kinnard!" a voice came from the door of the saloon. "What in blue blazes are you doin' rollin' around on the walk?"

Fargo glanced over and saw that a little banty rooster of a man had emerged from the saloon. He wore a brown tweed suit, a brocade vest, a white silk shirt, and a bright-red cravat with a fancy diamond stickpin in it. White hair hung almost to his shoulders, and a bristly white beard adorned his jutting chin.

"Get up from there!" he went on. "You're makin' a dadblamed fool of yourself!"

Fargo stepped back, lowered the hammer of his Colt, and slid the weapon back in its holster. He gave Hatchet-face—or Kinnard, as the white-bearded man called him—room to get up. For a moment, though, Kinnard didn't budge. He just lay there glaring daggers at Fargo. Then he wiped the back of his hand across his mouth, where a line of blood had trickled out. He must have bitten his tongue when he got hit, Fargo thought.

The bearded man came closer to Fargo and said, "Mister, if Kinnard here was givin' you trouble, I'm mighty sorry."

"No trouble," Fargo said with a little smile that had to be annoying to Kinnard. "Does he work for you?"

"Oh, no, but I sorta feel responsible for whatever goes on in Helldorado." The man hooked his thumbs in his vest and stuck out his chest like a pouter pigeon. "You see, it's my town."

Fargo raised an eyebrow. "You own the whole place, do you?"

"Well, not the whole place, o' course. Fact is, I don't

own nothin' but this here saloon. But it was my idea to put a town here, and I'm the mayor." The man unhooked his right thumb from his vest and stuck out his hand. "Ebeneezer Bates is the name. And you are . . . ?"

From the boardwalk, Kinnard said, "The bastard who's about to be dead!" He lunged for one of the fallen guns.

Fargo got there first, bringing the heel of his boot down on the back of Kinnard's hand. He didn't stomp hard enough to break any bones, but Kinnard yelled in pain anyway. Fargo used his other foot to send the Colt spinning away down the boardwalk, safely out of reach.

"Dadblast it, Kinnard, what did I tell you?" Ebeneezer Bates demanded hotly. "You know better'n to start raisin' a ruckus right outside my place." Bates glanced at Fargo. "I see to it that Helldorado is a nice, peaceful community, Mister . . . " He paused to give Fargo time to supply his last name.

Since that was the second time Bates had asked for his name, Fargo supplied it. "I'm called Skye Fargo," he said. He stepped back, taking his foot off Kinnard's hand. "And I'm not sure how welcome I feel in your town, Bates."

Bates took hold of Fargo's left arm and steered him toward the door of the saloon. "Well, you just come right on in here, son, and we'll see what we can do about changin' your opinion of Helldorado. The drinks're on me!"

Fargo didn't argue. He kept an eye on Kinnard, though, as Bates led him inside the saloon. The hatchet-faced gunman didn't try anything else. He just lay there on the boardwalk, glaring his hatred toward Fargo until the batwings had flapped shut behind the Trailsman and Mayor Bates.

The inside of the saloon was typical of hundreds of others Fargo had seen on the frontier, a big room with a bar along one side, and tables scattered around the sawdust-covered floor. A staircase on the other side of the room from the bar led up to the building's second story. Not much of the light from the oil lamps that lit the place reached the second floor, so the small balcony up there was left mostly in shadow. Quite a few men stood at the bar, and at least half of the tables were occupied. Later in the evening, the place probably would be even busier, but there was a pretty good crowd on hand. And all of them seemed to be hard-faced men who regarded Fargo with narrowed eyes. Fargo hadn't seen any women in Helldorado yet.

Bates still had a hand on Fargo's arm. Fargo didn't like being touched by strangers, but he tolerated it this time. A man like Bates might have valuable information, if he could be induced to part with it. "Come on over here to my private table," Bates said as he led Fargo across the room. To one of the bartenders working behind the hardwood, he called, "Art, bring over a bottle of the good stuff."

Bates's private table was covered with green baize. Cards were scattered on it, and a solitaire game was laid out. Bates must have been playing when the commotion on the boardwalk outside attracted his attention. He pulled out a chair for Fargo and said, "Sit yourself down, son."

Fargo started to take the seat, but then noted that if he did so, he would have his back to the rest of the room. Years of ingrained caution made him step around the table to pull out one of the other chairs. "This one will do me," he said as he sank down into it. There was nothing behind him here but a blank wall.

Bates pursed his lips, but he said, "That's fine, that's fine. Sit wherever you want, it don't matter." The bartender arrived with glasses and a bottle. Bates motioned curtly for him to put them down.

When the bartender was gone, Bates poured the drinks himself. He picked up his glass and said, "Welcome to Helldorado, Mr. Fargo. I hope you can forget about that little scrap."

Fargo sipped the whiskey. It was indeed "the good stuff," as Bates had said.

"Everybody gets a little proddy now and then. I reckon that fella Kinnard is no exception."

"I'll have a word with him," Bates said in a hard voice. "It won't happen again."

"I thought you said he didn't work for you."

"He don't. But folks around here listen to me when I talk. You see, this is—"

"Your town," Fargo finished for him.

Bates laughed. "Yeah, I reckon I tend to get a mite carried away with that. But I'm mighty proud of Helldorado. In my younger years, I thought I'd never find a place like this—so I had to start it up myself!" He tossed back the rest of the drink, then continued, "Gaily bedight, a gallant knight, in sunshine and in shadow, had journeyed along, singing a song, in search of Eldorado."

"Edgar Allen Poe," Fargo said.

Bates looked at him in surprise. "You know the fella?"

"But he grew old," Fargo said, "this knight so bold, and o'er his heart a shadow, fell as he found, no spot of ground, that looked like Eldorado."

Bates slapped the table and cackled in delight. "That was me, all right. Old and with a shadow over my heart, just like in the poem. And then I says to myself, if I can't find Eldorado, I'll just make my own."

"The town is called Helldorado," Fargo pointed out.

Bates waved a hand and said, "Just my little joke. It gets a mite wild an' woolly around here sometimes. We got a lot of men come through who still got all the bark on 'em. So I called it Helldorado. You're the first one who's understood, though. How'd you come to know Mr. Poe's poem?"

"I read a little now and then," Fargo explained, "and I've known men who memorized a lot of poems. I've heard that some of those fur trappers, back in the Shining Times, could recite most of Shakespeare's plays from memory. It was something to pass the time."

"I reckon so. I got me a book that has a bunch of Mr. Poe's rhymes in it. I read it sometimes of a night, the way some fellers read the Bible." Bates refilled their glasses. "Damn, I'm glad you come to Helldorado, Mr. Fargo!" He lowered his voice and leaned forward as he said,

"Most o' these old boys ain't got no culture at all." Bates picked up his glass. "To culture!"

"To culture," Fargo agreed.

And to stolen army rifles, he added silently.

7

"What brings you to Helldorado, Mr. Fargo?" Bates asked after a few more minutes of chatting about the town.

"Just drifting," Fargo replied, then added, "I thought I might run into a couple of friends of mine. I think they're in these parts somewhere."

"That so? What are their names?"

Fargo smiled. "Smith and Jones."

"Like that, is it?" Bates said with a chuckle. "Like I told you, we got some rough fellas passin' through here, and not all of 'em like to use their real monikers. This here Smith and Jones, what might they look like?"

"One of them is tall, with big shoulders and sort of a broad face. The other one's a lot shorter and scrawnier, with a big nose, a mustache, and not much hair on top of his head." Fargo had just described the two men who had tried to kill him on the docks at Omaha.

Bates tugged on his beard and frowned in thought for a moment, then said, "Sorry, that don't ring no bells. I reckon there's fellas around here who'd fit those descriptions, especially the big one, but I don't know of anybody who looks like that little one."

"It's not really important," Fargo said. "If I don't run into them here, I'll find them some other place."

"Yeah, that's usually the way it is." Bates started to refill Fargo's glass, but Fargo moved it before the saloonkeeper could splash whiskey into it. "Don't tell me you had enough!" Bates exclaimed.

"It's good," Fargo said, "but I don't want to muddle my brain."

"That's a wise man talkin'." Bates chuckled again. "O' course, if more hombres felt like you, I'd be out o' business in a month!"

"I don't think that's very likely."

"No, when a gent comes in from ridin' a long, lonely trail, he wants two things: a drink and a gal. I can provide both."

"Is that so? I haven't seen any women at all in Helldorado."

Bates pulled an oversized pocket watch from his vest and opened it to check the time. "My gals will be down before too much longer. You got to understand, things don't really start to pop hereabouts until after dark."

"What's the law situation here?" Fargo asked with a note of caution in his voice. "Are you the town marshal, too, as well as being the mayor and founder?"

"Haw! That's a good'un." Bates shook his head. "There's no marshal or sheriff in Helldorado. If folks got a problem, they take care of it theirselves, rather than lookin' to the law. And that's the way we like it."

Fargo nodded. "As long as that works."

"It works just fine, let me tell you. You won't hear nobody complainin', that's for sure." Bates got a calculating look in his eyes. "You ask a heap o' questions, Mr. Fargo."

"I'm just a naturally curious man," Fargo said, hoping that he hadn't overplayed his hand.

"Nothin' wrong with that . . . most of the time." Bates's voice had a harder edge to it now. "I got a feelin', though, that you knew the answers to most o' them questions before you even asked 'em."

"What makes you think that?"

"Come here from Omaha, didn't you?"

"That's right."

"And you didn't hear nothin' about Helldorado while you were there?"

"I heard that it was a good place to steer clear of, if you're a timid soul." Fargo smiled thinly. "Nobody's ever accused me of that."

Bates studied Fargo for a moment, then said, "Nope, I don't reckon they would. What else did you hear?"

"That Helldorado was a town that didn't care where you'd been or what you'd done," Fargo said, deciding to put some of his cards on the table. "Sounded like just the sort of place I wanted to visit."

"Did it now?"

Fargo reached for the bottle, poured another drink for himself. Bates didn't object despite Fargo's earlier refusal. "That's right."

"Left Omaha in a hurry, did you?"

Fargo just threw back the drink and didn't answer. He had decided to let Bates draw his own conclusions. And since Bates didn't seem to recognize his name, it was possible the saloonkeeper might get the idea that Fargo was a man on the dodge, just like a lot of the other men in Helldorado. That could turn out to be a healthy image to cultivate.

Apparently satisfied with Fargo's lack of a reply, Bates went on, "You handled Kinnard without much fuss."

"He wasn't worth much fuss," Fargo said.

"Don't get the wrong idea 'bout Kinnard. He looks like some sort o' dude, but he's good with them guns he wears. He's a dangerous gent, and he ain't the type to forget what happened out there."

"Are you saying he's liable to try to settle the score?"

"It could happen," Bates said.

"As long as he comes at me from the front, that's fine," Fargo said. "I don't cotton much to bushwhackers and backshooters, though."

"Just a friendly warnin' to keep your eyes open, that's all." Bates glanced up at the shadowy balcony and the staircase leading down from it. "Ah, here's the gals now."

Fargo turned his head enough to see three women

descending the stairs. They wore typically gaudy saloon girl outfits—short, spangled dresses, hose with garters, and feathers in their hair. Two of them were getting a little long in the tooth, while the younger one had crossed eyes and no chin to speak of. Fargo didn't find any of them the least bit attractive. Judging by the whoops and hollers of the men in the saloon, though, most of them didn't share Fargo's opinion. They seemed thrilled to see the soiled doves.

Since he wasn't, Fargo pushed his empty glass aside and stood up. "I'd better go see to my horse," he said. "Thanks for the hospitality."

"You come back any time," Bates said. He laughed. "Drinks won't be on the house next time, though."

Fargo nodded and turned to walk out. He went past the bar where the three women already had men flocking around them, offering to buy them drinks.

When he pushed through the batwings and stepped onto the boardwalk, Fargo saw that night had fallen in Helldorado. He looked one way along the street and then the other, but he didn't see any sign of Kinnard. The gunman likely had slunk off somewhere to nurse the grudge that he now carried against Fargo.

After untying the Ovaro's reins, Fargo led the stallion down the street toward the town's only livery stable. It was next to the blacksmith shop, which was dark now, the smith probably having gone home. Light came through the open double doors of the stable, though.

As he walked along the street, Fargo pondered what he had learned so far in Helldorado. It wasn't much except that there was no law in the town, and he had known that already. He had the feeling, though, that Ebeneezer Bates had had just such a setup in mind when he'd founded Helldorado. Fargo knew how it usually worked in places like that: Outlaws were welcomed and offered a safe haven from the authorities, as long as they forked over a share of the loot from their crimes. As the mayor and owner of the largest saloon in town, Bates was probably in line for the biggest payoffs. It was an easy, relatively safe way to rake in a fortune in ill-gotten gains. Bates might not have any direct connection with the gang that had stolen those army rifles, but Fargo thought it was a safe bet that the thieves had been to Helldorado.

They might even be in town tonight, for all he knew.

That thought, and the fact that the gunman called Kinnard was out there somewhere, filled with murderous resentment, kept Fargo alert and on edge as he approached the livery stable. He led the Ovaro through the open doors and called out, "Anybody home?"

A tall, skinny old man with a battered felt hat pushed back on a head as bald as an egg sauntered out of the tack room and said, "Howdy there, mister. Got a horse you need to put up for the night?" The liveryman's prominent Adam's apple jumped up and down as he spoke.

"That's right," Fargo said. "Got any stalls open?"

"One or two. We'll be full up 'fore the night's over, though." The man came closer, his eyes widening in appreciation as he looked at the stallion. "That's a mighty nice-lookin' horse. I never seen one like that before, black on both ends and white in the middle. What do you call it?"

Fargo patted the stallion's shoulder. "He's an Ovaro."

"Mighty nice," the liveryman said again. "I'll take good care of him, mister." He turned to point. "Just put him in that stall over yonder. I'll get some grain for the trough."

When Fargo had the stallion unsaddled and in the stall, the liveryman dumped a bucket of grain in the feed trough. The water trough was already full. Fargo stepped out into the center aisle, and the bald man swung the stall door closed.

"Name's Hank Jessup," the man said, introducing himself. "This is my place, if you're wonderin'. I ain't got no hostler, do all the work myself. I'm a heap more spry than I look."

Fargo shook hands with him. "Pleased to meet you, Hank. I'm called Fargo."

"Pleasure's all mine, Mr. Fargo. 'Tain't often I get a customer in here who ain't an owlhoot."

Fargo frowned. "How do you know I'm not on the dodge?"

"Shoot, when a fella sees them hardcases all the time, he gets to where he can recognize 'em without no trouble. No offense, Mr. Fargo, but you look like an honest man to me."

Fargo grinned. Only in a place like Helldorado would a man worry about giving offense by calling another man honest. Feeling an instinctive liking for Hank Jessup, Fargo said, "Tell me about this town. It looks pretty rough to me."

"Oh, it is. Don't get me wrong. There's some law-abidin' folks around here, but they're outnumbered. That's the way Mayor Bates wants it. He makes a heap more money off owlhoots than he does off honest people."

Fargo nodded. "That's the feeling I had, too. You know a man named Kinnard?"

Hank let out a low whistle. "Ever'body knows Kinnard. Them that's got a lick o' sense know to steer clear of him, too."

"I guess I don't have a lick of sense, then," Fargo said with a grin. "I got into a fracas with him first thing when I rode into town."

Hank goggled at him. "*You're* the fella who knocked him down? I heard all about that. He come in here to get his horse, and he was spittin' and cussin' and sayin' how he was goin' to kill you."

"I've been threatened before," Fargo said.

"Kinnard's a mighty bad one, though. Mighty fast with a gun." Hank rubbed his jaw, which was bristly with white stubble. "Not as bad as Donohue, o' course."

"Who's Donohue?"

"Patch Donohue, they call him, on account of he wears a patch over one eye. Kinnard rides for him."

"Donohue has a ranch?" Fargo asked, hoping to sound naïve.

"No, when I say Kinnard rides for him, I mean he's a member of Donohue's gang. Worst bunch in the whole territory."

"Is that so?" Fargo said, trying not to sound too interested.

"Yep. If you got Kinnard gunnin' for you, Mr. Fargo, odds are you'll have to watch out for Donohue and the rest o' them owlhoots, too."

Fargo shook his head. "If it's as bad as all that, I'm surprised the army hasn't come in to clean up the area."

"Army. Huh!" Hank snorted in contempt. "They got better things to do. Got Injuns to worry about. They stay out on patrol all the time, tryin' to make sure no war parties slip through to bother the wagon trains. Shoot, somebody stole a bunch o' guns from the army 'bout a week ago, and they can't find hide nor hair of 'em!"

"Seems like I heard something about that."

Hank took a pipe from his vest pocket and started to fill it from a tobacco pouch he wore on a string around his neck. "Yeah, after it happened the army sent a patrol over here to poke around, but the young feller in charge of it, he just asked the mayor a few questions and then went away. The mayor told that pup he didn't know nothin' 'bout any stolen guns, and the young feller believed him!"

"Was there a sergeant with that patrol, a big fella without any hair?"

Hank grinned, put his pipe in his mouth, then took off his hat and ran his other hand over his smooth scalp. "Yes, sir, he was as bald as me but a heap uglier. You know him?"

"We've crossed paths," Fargo said.

So Lieutenant Ross and Sergeant Creed had been to Helldorado. Colonel Barrett had mentioned that someone from the army had ridden over here to question the citizens after the raid on the supply wagons, but he hadn't said that it had been Ross's troop. From what Fargo had seen of the young officer so far, he thought Barrett was placing too much faith in Ross. It would be just a fluke if the lieutenant ever turned up those missing rifles.

On the other hand, maybe Barrett had started to realize that. Maybe that was why he had been so anxious to enlist the Trailsman in the effort to track down the thieves.

"Say, Mr. Fargo, you're a mighty curious feller," Hank commented. "I hope I ain't spoke out of turn about anything."

"Not at all," Fargo assured him. "I like to know as much as I can about a place, even when I'm just passing through."

"Are you just passin' through Helldorado? Or do you plan to stay awhile?"

"I guess that depends. I'm looking for a couple of men. Maybe you know them." Once again, Fargo described the two killers who had come after him in Omaha. Of course, he knew where they were—in pauper's graves in the town cemetery—but no one else in Helldorado had to know that.

He could tell from Hank's reaction as he spoke that the liveryman recognized the description of the two men. "That little weasely one is called Burgess," Hank said when Fargo was finished. "The big one's Merritt."

"You've seen them around town, then?"

"Not for several days, now that I think on it. But they been here plenty, all right. They ride for Patch Donohue, just like Kinnard." Hank squinted at the Trailsman. "Say, Mr. Fargo, I didn't misjudge you, now did I? You ain't a outlaw like all these other fellers you been talkin' about?"

"I'm not an outlaw," Fargo said. He was willing to allow Ebeneezer Bates to believe otherwise, but he didn't want to lie to Hank, who seemed to be a straight shooter.

"Then how come you're lookin' for Burgess and Merritt?"

"Personal business," Fargo said. It was a curt answer, but one that almost any Westerner would accept without question.

Hank Jessup did just that. He nodded and said, "If I see 'em around, you want me to let you know?"

The old man wasn't going to be seeing the two dead hardcases in Helldorado or anywhere else, but Fargo nodded anyway. "I'd appreciate that," he said. "I have just one more question."

"Go right ahead."

"Where's the best place to stay in Helldorado? I didn't see a hotel or a boarding house when I rode in."

"That's 'cause there ain't any. Most o' the saloons rent out rooms, though." Hank jerked a thumb upward. "Or there's my hayloft. It ain't fancy, but I ain't sure but what it's cleaner than most o' them saloons."

That sounded like a good idea to Fargo. He said, "How much do you charge?"

"Shoot, I'll throw it in with the bill for that black-and-white hoss. The hay's already up there, whether anybody's sleepin' in it or not."

Fargo nodded. "All right, you've got yourself a deal." He told himself that when he left Helldorado, he would throw in a little extra money for Hank, whether the old man wanted it or not. "I'll get my gear and turn in."

"You ain't goin' back out to the saloons?"

"It was a long day," Fargo said. "I'm tired."

"You really ain't the usual sort we get here in Helldorado. Those boys don't stop carousin' until after midnight."

"Well, I need my sleep."

"I'll be down here all night. I'll see that you ain't disturbed."

Fargo nodded his thanks and fetched his saddlebags and the Henry rifle from the stall where the Ovaro was eating the grain in the feed trough. He considered himself lucky that he had been able to strike up a friendship so quickly with one of Helldorado's few honest citizens.

Unless Hank Jessup wasn't as honest as he made himself out to be, Fargo thought as he climbed the ladder to the hayloft. He didn't think that was the case though— he was a good judge of character and believed that Hank was just what he seemed to be—but nothing could be ruled out at this point, Fargo knew. Until he had definite proof, he had to be a little suspicious of everyone he met.

Enough light came from the lantern hanging in the stable's center aisle for Fargo to see in the hayloft. He set his saddlebags and rifle aside, took off his hat and boots and gunbelt, and kicked together enough of the loose hay to form a comfortable bed. As he stretched out on the hay, he put his hands behind his head and laced his fingers together. He was tired, as he had told Hank, but before dozing off he wanted to think some more about what he had learned. From what the old liveryman had told him, Patch Donohue was the man most likely to be behind the deadly raid on the army supply wagons and the theft of the rifles. Such an atrocity would require a large, well-organized gang, and evidently that was what Donohue headed up. There was also the connection between Donohue and the two men who had tried to kill Fargo in Omaha. Fargo warned himself not to jump to conclusions, but he had to admit that all the evidence pointed to Donohue.

Besides, the men who had ambushed and murdered those soldiers were cold-blooded killers. Kinnard, also one of Donohue's men, seemed to fit that description, and Fargo knew for sure that Burgess and Merritt did.

He was going to have to meet this Patch Donohue, Fargo concluded. He hadn't quite figured out how yet, but that would come to him.

He rolled onto his side, ready to go to sleep. As he did so, he heard a horse walk by in the street outside. There was nothing unusual about that, but some instinct brought Fargo to his feet and sent him over to the doors through which hay could be lifted into the loft. He found the latch and eased one of them open a bit, then knelt beside the narrow crack to peer down into the street.

The rider moving past the stable was hunched over in the saddle as if exhausted. In the darkness, Fargo couldn't tell much about him other than that he was small in stature and wore a broad-brimmed hat pulled down over his face. Fargo frowned, remembering the rider that had shadowed him out of Omaha. Fargo had no way of knowing for sure if the rider going past the stable was the same one who had followed him, but it was at least a possibility. The man had come into town from the right direction.

The rider moved on out of sight. Fargo committed to memory as much as he could about the man and his horse, which wasn't much because of the darkness, but he thought he might recognize both of them if he saw them again.

He went back to the pile of hay, stretched out on it, and was sound asleep in a matter of minutes.

8

Fargo didn't know how long he had been asleep, and at first he had no idea what had roused him from his slumber. But in a matter of split seconds, his keenly honed senses told him what was wrong. He smelled smoke, and he heard the ugly sound of a fist thudding into flesh. Several horses let out shrill trumpets of fear, no doubt because they smelled the smoke, too.

He rolled over, grabbing the Colt from the holster beside him as he did so. Reaching the edge of the loft, he peered down and saw the hatchet-faced gunman Kinnard holding up Hank Jessup by the shirtfront. Hank's face had streaks of blood on it. Kinnard's other fist was cocked beside his ear, poised to slam another blow into Hank's face. Off to one side, flames licked at some of the straw that was scattered around the barn.

"Damn it, old man!" Kinnard shouted. "His horse is here! Tell me where the bastard is, or I'll leave you here to burn!"

"The bastard's up here, Kinnard!" Fargo called down as he lined the Colt on the scrawny gunman.

Kinnard whipped around, twisting his body so that he could look up at the loft. He still had hold of the liveryman. Fargo held off on the revolver's trigger because he didn't want to risk hitting Hank. Kinnard's right hand dropped to his hip and jerked out the gun at his side. He tipped up the barrel and fired.

Fargo leaped back as Kinnard's bullet sizzled past him. He was acutely aware of all the dangers he was facing here. Kinnard kept firing, sending slugs punching up through the planks that formed the loft. Not only that, but with a fire burning below as well, there was a good chance the whole barn would become an inferno in a matter of minutes. If Fargo wanted to save himself, not to mention Hank and all the horses in the stalls below, he had to get out of here.

He kicked the hay doors open and flung himself out into space, remembering what he had seen when he looked out through them earlier: A sturdy beam was attached to the wall of the barn, with a block and tackle arrangement on it to lift bundles of hay. Fargo's left hand caught hold of the rope. It was tied off, so he didn't drop all the way to the ground. Instead he fell only a couple of feet before he was brought up with a jolt that sent pain through his arm and shoulder. But now he was close enough to the ground so that he could let go and drop the rest of the way. He did so, ignoring the pain in his arm, and landed lightly on his bare feet, bending his knees to lessen the impact against the ground. From here he could see into the barn, where Kinnard was emptying both of his revolvers into the loft. The gunman had let go of Hank Jessup, who was slumped on the ground, apparently only half conscious. Beyond Kinnard, the fire was spreading quickly, the flames now licking at the rear wall of the barn.

"Kinnard!" Fargo shouted. The killer spun toward him, both guns still spitting lead. Under the circumstances, his shots were remarkably accurate. The bullets tore through the air where Fargo's upper chest would have been if he had been standing upright.

But the Trailsman was still in a crouch, so the slugs went over his head as he squeezed off two shots of his own. The Colt bucked hard against his palm as he fired.

As both of Fargo's shots bored into his chest, Kinnard flew backward like a puppet jerked on a string. He landed on his back, arms outflung to the sides. Fargo surged to his feet and ran into the barn, keeping the Colt trained on the fallen gunman just in case. Kinnard was dead, though, Fargo saw as he reached his side. Kinnard's dark eyes were open and staring sightlessly at the roof of the barn.

Fargo turned to Hank Jessup and bent to get hold of the elderly liveryman. He slid an arm around Hank and lifted him with ease. Hank was mumbling incoherently. Fargo said, "Come on! We've got to get out of here!"

"Th—the horses!" Hank managed to choke out.

"I'll turn them loose!" Fargo ran Hank toward the entrance, and then, halfway there, gave him a push that sent the old man stumbling on out into the night.

Over the crackling of the flames, Fargo heard shouting from the street. People had noticed the fire and would be running to help put it out. Fargo didn't think they would be in time to save the building. He hurried from stall to stall, throwing open the gates and letting the panicked horses race out, away from the fire and smoke. The Ovaro was the only one that didn't stampede; instead the big stallion pushed at Fargo with its head as if he was trying to make Fargo run out of the barn first.

"Go on!" Fargo snapped. "Get out of here!"

The Ovaro hesitated again, then turned and ran out of the barn. Fargo checked the progress of the fire and scrambled up the ladder to the loft. He thought he had time to get his gear.

Smoke coiled around his head and made him cough. His eyes smarted from its acrid sting. He reached the loft and pulled himself off the ladder. Grabbing up his saddlebags and the Henry rifle, he tossed them through the open hay doors. His hat and boots went next. That left his gunbelt. He snatched it up, jammed the Colt back in the holster, and looped the belt over his shoulder. When he stumbled over to the ladder, he recoiled at the blistering heat that rose into his face. The fire had reached the bottom of the ladder. If he climbed down now, he would be descending into the flames. That meant he had to go out the hay doors again.

Wracked by coughing, Fargo dropped to his knees and crawled over to the opening. He wasn't sure he could leap out and grab hold of the rope again. His head was spinning, and he was beginning to be disoriented. He had to get out now or risk being overcome by the smoke.

Fargo toppled out into the darkness.

Falling was the last thing he remembered for a while. Later, when he regained consciousness, he couldn't recall landing in the street. But the aches and pains that filled his body told their own eloquent story.

He tried to move, and a fresh wave of pain went through him. A hand touched his shoulder, pressing him down, and a familiar voice said, "Hold on there, hoss. Don't go to movin' around just yet, in case somethin's broke that I don't know about yet."

Fargo kept his eyes closed and lay there—wherever *there* was—while stiff fingers poked and prodded at him. Several times, the rough examination provoked a groan from him. Finally, the fingers went away, and the same voice said, "Reckon nothin's busted or ruptured, just mighty bruised. You're a lucky man, Fargo."

Fargo had recognized the voice by now. He forced his eyes open and looked up into the weathered, bearded face of Ebeneezer Bates. The saloonkeeper and mayor of Helldorado was smiling as he bent next to the cot where Fargo lay, but the smile didn't reach Bates's eyes. They were hard and grim.

"Where am I?" Fargo grated out.

"Back room o' my saloon," Bates replied. "I had the boys bring you over here after you fell out o' Hank Jessup's hayloft. Accordin' to Hank, you saved his life. Saved all the horses in the stable, too. Folks are mighty grateful to you for that."

"The old man . . . Jessup . . . he's all right?"

"Bunged up a mite, like you, but he'll be fine. You're both in a hell of a lot better shape than Kinnard. Fried to a crisp, he was."

"He was dead before that," Fargo said. He pushed himself up onto an elbow, ignoring the anvil chorus that started playing in his head when he did so, and looked around the room. There was a desk on one side, probably where Bates did his bookkeeping, and the other side of the room was filled with stacks of crates containing bottles of liquor. Evidently this room did triple duty as office, sleeping quarters, and storage room.

"Ventilated him, did you? I figured as much from what old Hank said. He told us Kinnard came in there and knocked the lantern over and started handin' him a beatin', all because your horse was in one of the stalls and he was lookin' for you." Bates shook his head. "Kinnard never did have any sense. He was so full o' hate he couldn't think of anything except settlin' his score with you."

Fargo sat up on the cot and swung his bare feet to the floor. He looked at Bates's desk and saw his saddlebags, hat, and gunbelt piled on top of it. His Henry rifle leaned in the corner behind the desk. Next to the rifle sat his boots.

"Thanks for taking care of my gear," he said.

Bates waved a hand. "Glad to do it. Like I said, the whole town's grateful to you for savin' them horses."

"I guess the barn burned down?"

Bates nodded and said, "Plumb to the ground. Don't know what old Hank will do now. He lost everything."

And he was partially to blame for that, Fargo thought. If he hadn't gone to Hank's in the first place, Kinnard wouldn't have come there looking for him. Of course, there was really only one man who bore true responsibility for what had happened. That was Kinnard himself. And he had paid the ultimate price for his hate.

"I reckon my saddle burned up in the barn."

"Yep. You can buy another saddle, though. Got a couple for sale down at the general store. Be a lot easier to replace than if you'd lost that fine repeatin' rifle. Or that horse."

Fargo came to his feet, paying no attention to the dizziness that went through him. "Where is my horse?"

"Tied to the hitch rail outside. That's where all the critters that we were able to round up are. A few of 'em bolted so hard that nobody was able to catch 'em. Not that stallion o' yours, though. After you fell out of the loft, he went right to your side and stayed there, lookin' out for you. I didn't think at first he was goin' to let us get to you so's we could doctor you. After a while he seemed to get the idea that we didn't mean you no harm, though."

Fargo nodded. He wasn't surprised the Ovaro had stood guard over him. This wasn't the first time such a thing had happened.

He stepped over to the desk and picked up his gunbelt. As he buckled it on, Bates said, "Hold on there! What're you doin', Fargo? You don't need that smoke pole right now."

"Kinnard had friends," Fargo said as he bent slightly to tie down the holster. "They're liable to come after me as soon as word gets around that I killed him, if it hasn't already."

"Nobody's goin' to bother you here," Bates insisted. "Nobody would dare——"

As if to give the lie to his words, heavy footsteps suddenly sounded outside the door, and a booted foot kicked it open. A huge form filled the doorway, and a deep voice bellowed, "Where is he? Where's the hydrophobic skunk who killed Kinnard?"

Fargo's fingers curled around the walnut grips of his Colt, but he didn't draw the revolver as he turned to face the newcomer. The man wore a black hat with a steepled crown, a black-and-white cowhide vest over a gray woolen shirt, and black whipcord trousers over black boots. His face under the broad brim of the hat was craggy, and a black mustache hung down over both corners of his wide mouth. His right eye squinted at Fargo. The left one was covered with a black patch attached to a cord that tied around his head.

Fargo knew he was looking at Patch Donohue. The only question was whether or not he would be swapping lead with the man in the next few seconds.

"Dadblast it, Patch!" Bates burst out. "You can't come bullin' in here like that! This is my place!"

"Shut up, you old fool!" Donohue grated. His lone eye glared at Fargo. "You're him, ain't you?"

"I killed Kinnard, if that's what you mean," Fargo replied coolly. He was calling on his reserves of strength to keep him steady and help him ignore the results of all the battering his body had endured over the past week. The ride from Omaha to Helldorado had given him the chance to recuperate from the earlier brawls, but now he was beaten up again. No one could tell that, though, from the way he stood tall and straight, ready to meet whatever threat Patch Donohue might represent.

"Gunned him in a fair fight, did you?" Donohue growled.

"He was shooting at me first, if that's what you mean," Fargo said. "I don't know how fair it was, though, because Kinnard was a hothead and an idiot."

Abruptly, Donohue laughed, giving out with a hoarse bray of amusement that filled the room. "That's sure enough true! He was hellacious fast, but he needed somebody to do his thinking for him most of the time."

Donohue tucked his thumbs behind his belt and relaxed. Fargo kept his hand on the butt of his gun just in case the outlaw was trying to lull him into a fatal mistake. He said, "So you don't aim to settle the score for Kinnard?"

"He made up his own mind to go after you, mister. He paid his own price."

"Do the rest of Kinnard's friends feel the same way?"

"They feel the way I tell 'em to feel!" Donohue roared. "They ride for me, just like Kinnard did. If I tell 'em to lay off, they lay off."

"Is that what you're going to tell them?" Fargo asked.

"Maybe." Donohue reached up and tugged on one end of his mustache. "What's your name, mister?"

Bates supplied the answer, saying, "This here is Skye Fargo, Patch."

Donohue grunted. "Name's familiar, but I don't place you right off-hand, mister. Ever been to Texas?"

"I've been most places west of the Mississippi, and a few east of there," Fargo replied.

"Yeah, I get around a mite, too. But I plan to stay here in Nebraska Territory for a while. What about you?"

"Depends on what I find to keep me here," Fargo said.

"How about a job?" Donohue said. "With Kinnard dead, I need another good man. I figure the gent who killed him has to be better'n him."

Fargo frowned. He had let Ebeneezer Bates think that he might be an outlaw, but now he had a chance to assume the role fully. The idea of riding with Donohue's gang was repugnant to Fargo, but he figured he could stand it for a while if it meant he would have a better chance of finding out what had happened to the stolen army rifles.

He didn't want to appear too eager, though. He said, "I didn't come to Helldorado looking for work."

"Sometimes chances turn up that we ain't expecting," Donohue pointed out.

Fargo couldn't argue with that. But neither did he want to rush into anything. He said, "Let me think about it."

"Don't think too long," Donohue said, a hard edge creeping into his voice. "My boys will be more likely to forget about Kinnard if you're one of us."

"I'll keep that in mind."

"You do that." Donohue gave Bates a curt nod, then swung around and stalked out of the room, kicking the door shut behind him with his heel.

Bates blew out a long sigh. "Damned if I didn't think you boys were about to go at it," he said. "I was ready to dive behind that desk when the shootin' started."

"You didn't expect Donohue to offer me a job, did you?"

"Hell, no." Bates tugged on his beard. "Now that I think on it, though, I ain't overmuch surprised. You know what they say about honor among thieves, and Donohue is just about the biggest crook in these parts."

"Is that so? The two of you seemed almost friendly."

Bates drew himself up and tried to look dignified. "I'm a businessman. I got to get along with all sorts o' folks if I want to make a livin'. I don't care what Donohue and his boys do anywhere else, as long as they behave theirselves in Helldorado."

Fargo nodded. He sat down on the cot and pulled his boots on. "I need some rest. This has been a hell of a night."

"Where'll you go?" Bates wanted to know. "You were sleepin' in the hayloft down at Hank's place, but it ain't there no more." His bushy eyebrows jumped as he indicated the second floor with a bob of his head. "I got rooms to rent upstairs. And one of the gals to go with it if you want."

Fargo thought about the three soiled doves he had seen earlier and shook his head. "No thanks."

"To the room, the gal, or both?"

"The girl," Fargo said. "I'll take the room. Sleep is what I need."

"Sure, I understand."

"When do you think Donohue will want his answer?"

"He'll probably hang around town tonight," Bates said, "and tomorrow he'll come see you again. If he don't like what you got to tell him, there'll be trouble."

"I'll have to think on that, then," Fargo said.

"You do that." Bates turned toward the door. "Come on. I'll show you where you can sleep."

A short time later, Fargo was alone in one of the saloon's upstairs rooms. Along the way, all three of the saloon girls had offered to accompany him, and they had all looked disappointed when he turned them down. He really did want some rest, though, and even if they had been more attractive, he would have refused the offer of their company. He also wanted to sort out these new developments, and if he was going to do that, he didn't need any distractions.

The room was small, furnished only with a narrow bed, a small table, and a single chair. The window had an oilcloth shade over it. Fargo didn't bother lighting the lamp on the table next to the bed. He just placed his Colt on the table next to the lamp, laid the Henry rifle on the floor next to the bed, and stretched out on top of the blanket with his gunbelt and boots still on. If there was any more trouble tonight, he was going to be ready for it.

As he stared up at the darkened ceiling, he thought about everything that had happened. Kinnard coming after him like that made sense, at least from the twisted point of view of the hatchet-faced gunman. Nothing else did, though. Fargo was not so full of himself that he found it hard to believe Bates and Donohue didn't know he was the Trailsman. The frontier was a big place, and it was entirely credible that neither man would recognize the name.

But Burgess and Merritt, the two hardcases who had come after him in Omaha, had ridden with Donohue's gang. Why in blazes would they have tried to kill him if they hadn't known who he was and figured that Colonel Barrett was trying to get him to help the army?

Maybe Burgess and Merritt *had* recognized him, Fargo thought with narrowed eyes, but they hadn't warned Donohue about him before trying to kill him on the docks. If that was the case, it was conceivable that Donohue didn't know who he was and didn't have any idea of the connection between Fargo and the army. And with Burgess and Merritt both dead, they couldn't tip off the boss outlaw. It would be quite a stroke of luck if things had worked out that way, but Fargo knew it was possible.

And with the odds facing him in Helldorado, Fargo thought as he dozed off for the second time tonight, he was prepared to accept all the luck he could get.

9

Fargo woke up to peace and quiet for a change. Light coming around the edges of the oilcloth shade over the window told him it was morning. He sat up, swung his legs out of bed, and stood, grimacing as sore muscles sent little jolts of discomfort stabbing through him. He pulled the chamber pot from under the bed, took care of that, and put on his hat and gunbelt to go downstairs.

The saloon was open, but the only customers were a couple of drunks who were dozing face down at two of the tables. A lone bartender was behind the hardwood, yawning and wiping off the bar with a dirty rag. When he saw Fargo coming down the stairs, he lifted a hand in greeting.

"The boss said to tell you that he's over at the hash house, eatin' breakfast," the bartender said. "He wanted you to join him if you got up in time."

"Where would that be?" Fargo asked.

The bartender pointed. "Catty-corner across the street. Place is called Cullum's."

Fargo nodded his thanks and went out, pushing through the batwings onto the boardwalk. The morning was already warm. It was going to be another hot, sultry day.

Spotting Cullum's across the street, Fargo stepped down off the planks. A few people were moving in Helldorado, but overall the settlement was drowsy and barely stirring this morning. Fargo paused beside the Ovaro and patted the stallion's flank. "Sorry you had to spend the night tied to a hitch rail," he murmured to the horse.

Before heading toward the hash house, Fargo cast a keen eye over the rest of the animals tied at the rails along the street. There were quite a few of them, since the horses from Hank Jessup's stable were tethered to the rails, as well as the mounts that normally would have been left there overnight by men passed out in the saloons. Fargo was searching for the horse he had seen plodding into town late the night before, carrying the mysterious rider who had followed him from Omaha. It was well nigh hopeless, though. He hadn't gotten a good enough look at the horse to recognize it after all.

Fargo walked across the street, stepped up onto the boardwalk, and went into Cullum's. "Fargo!" Ebeneezer Bates called from one of the tables. "Over here."

Fargo moved across the room to join the mayor. He nodded and said, "Good morning."

"Mornin'," Bates replied. "Sleep well?"

"Nobody else tried to kill me, if that's what you mean."

Bates chuckled. "I reckon that's always a good thing."

Fargo pulled out one of the empty chairs, dropped his hat on the table, and sat down. A heavy-set man in an apron came out from behind the counter and walked over to the table. "What'll it be, mister?" he asked.

Fargo looked at Bates's plate, which was piled high with slices of ham, hash browns, fried eggs, and biscuits. "I'll have what the mayor is having," he told the man in the apron.

"Comin' up. Coffee?"

"Plenty of it, and black as sin," Fargo said. When the man had gone back behind the counter to call out the order to the cook in the kitchen, Fargo went on to Bates, "Seen Donohue this morning?"

The mayor shook his head. "It's too early for that scalawag to be up and about. He did a heap o' drinkin' last night, then went down to the bordello and got hisself a pair of gals. Plumb wore hisself out, from what I've heard."

"You seem to know just about everything that goes on around here."

Bates snorted. "I ought to. I spread around enough *dinero* to keep informed."

It came as no surprise to Fargo that Bates had his finger on the pulse of Helldorado. There was a chance Bates knew exactly where those stolen rifles were. It would simplify matters if Fargo could put a gun to his head and make him talk, but he was convinced that Bates was stubborn enough not to crack. Such a move would also reveal that Fargo was working with the army and ruin any chance he might have of finding out anything from Donohue. It was better to be patient, Fargo told himself.

The food he had ordered arrived at the table a few minutes later, and he dug in. He washed down the meal with several cups of strong black coffee. By the time he had finished and pushed away his empty plate, Fargo felt halfway human again, though he would still be carrying around some aches and pains for several days. He drained the last of the coffee from his cup.

Bates had finished his breakfast several minutes earlier and was lingering over his coffee. He said, "You made up your mind what you're goin' to tell Donohue?"

Fargo didn't answer directly. He said, "It seems to me a man could get his hands on considerable cash by riding with Donohue."

"I reckon that's true enough. Him and his boys always seem to be flush. Sometimes, though, when they ride off not all of 'em come back."

"All of life is a risk," Fargo said with a smile.

"Yeah, but it's more risky when you ride with fellas who smell like gun smoke."

"I'll take my chances."

Bates nodded. "Somehow I figured you would."

Fargo picked up the coffeepot, shook it to see if any was left, then set it aside. "Where's the old man from the livery stable?" he asked. "I feel sort of responsible for what happened to him. I'd like to be sure he's all right."

"The blacksmith took him in. They're friends, what with their places bein' right next to each other like that."

"I think I'll stop by and see him." Fargo got to his feet and reached into his pocket for a coin to pay for his meal.

"Never you mind about that," Bates told him. "Breakfast is on me."

"You're mighty generous. You bought me drinks last night."

"Consider it all a welcome to Helldorado's newest citizen."

Fargo nodded his thanks and left the eatery. He didn't tell Bates that he didn't intend to be one of Helldorado's citizens for any longer than was absolutely necessary.

Smoke curled from the chimney of the blacksmith shop, and Fargo could hear the ringing of hammer on anvil as he approached. He paused to look grimly at the heap of smoking rubble where the livery barn had stood, then shook his head and stepped into the open doorway of the squat building made from blocks of sod. A burly man in a thick leather apron was at the anvil hammering out a horseshoe. The smith had a tangled black beard and wore a battered derby hat perched on a rumpled thatch of black hair. He looked up at Fargo and gave a curt nod of greeting.

"Something I can do for you?"

"I was told Hank Jessup is here," Fargo said. "I'd like to see him."

The smith dropped the hot shoe he had been working on into a bucket of water, causing a hiss of steam. He set his hammer aside and said, "I recognize you. You're the fella who was sleeping in Hank's loft when all the commotion started."

"That's right," Fargo admitted. He wondered if the smith was going to blame him for what had happened to the livery stable. It would be understandable if he did.

The man jerked a blunt thumb over his shoulder. "Hank's in the back. Go on ahead."

"Much obliged," Fargo said as he started past.

"By the way, my name's Bert Abbott."

"Pleased to meet you, Bert. I'm called Fargo."

"Yeah," Abbott said. "I know."

Fargo felt the man's narrowed gaze watching him as he proceeded on through the blacksmith shop and came out into a small yard between the shop and a cabin that was also made of sod. Hank Jessup sat in a rocking chair in front of the cabin. He looked up at the Trailsman with a grin and said, "Good mornin', Mr. Fargo. How are you?"

Fargo studied the bruises on the old man's face. "In about the same shape as you, Hank," he said. "Beat up a mite."

"Oh, I've had it worse'n this," Hank said with a wave of his hand. "Leastways that bastard Kinnard didn't pistol-whip me. I was afraid he might, he was so crazy-mad."

Fargo hunkered on his heels next to the rocking chair and said, "I'm sorry I brought trouble down on your head, Hank. Sorry about your barn."

Hank shook his head. "Don't trouble yourself over it, Mr. Fargo. There weren't no way you could've known what Kinnard was goin' to do. Might as well try to guess what a mad dog will do, or where lightning'll strike. Things like that just happen."

"Well, you're being mighty reasonable about it, I'll say that for you," Fargo told the old man with a grin. "If there's anything I can do to make it up to you, just say the word."

"Well . . ." Hank's leathery forehead creased in a frown. "I was thinkin' I might leave Helldorado."

"You need some traveling money?" Fargo didn't have much cash, but he was willing to give as much as he could to Hank.

The old man shook his head. "No, I got a little saved up, and I didn't lose it in the fire." He lowered his voice and leaned closer to Fargo. "I got it buried in a coffee can, out back o' the place where the barn used to be. So don't you worry about that."

"What can I do for you, then?"

"Maybe you know of some place I can get work. A

friend of yours, maybe, who'd hire on an old man, even if it's out of pity."

"Pity, hell!" Fargo exclaimed. "I heard you say you ran that stable all by yourself. I expect you could work a lot of younger men right into the ground."

"I always have been a hard worker," Hank admitted.

Fargo glanced around. No one was in earshot except Hank. Inside the smithy, Bert Abbott was hammering on the anvil again. Fargo said quietly, "Go to Omaha and see Colonel Barrett at army headquarters there. Tell him I said for him to see about finding work for you. He's in charge of the whole Department of the Platte, so I reckon there's plenty he needs done."

Hank's eyes widened. "I always thought I'd like to work for the cavalry someday," he said. "Wouldn't I have to join the army, though? I'm a mite old for that."

Fargo chuckled. "I think the colonel can find a position for you as a civilian worker. How's that sound?"

"Mighty good." Hank put out his hand. "I'm much obliged to you, Mr. Fargo."

"It's the least I can do," Fargo said as he shook hands with the old man.

He chatted with Hank for a few minutes longer, then left the blacksmith shop and walked down Helldorado's main street. It was time he found Patch Donohue and gave the outlaw chief an answer to the question Donohue had asked the night before.

Before he could do so, however, a warning instinct kicked in and made him look around. About half a block behind him, a figure ducked into the narrow space between two buildings. Fargo caught only a glimpse of whoever it was, but he saw enough to recognize the diminutive figure and the floppy-brimmed hat. That was the same person who had ridden into Helldorado late the night before, after following him from Omaha.

Fargo stood there for a second, eyes narrowed in thought. Helldorado wasn't a very big place. He could go after the skulker and have a reasonable chance of finding him. Or he could sit back and wait for the follower to come to him. That might be an even more effective way of finding out what the hombre was up to. Fargo turned and walked on, his senses alert. Though he didn't turn around to look, he felt sure the watcher was still back there behind him, keeping an eye on him.

Bates had said that Donohue was at the bordello the night before, after leaving the saloon. Chances were the big outlaw was still there. Fargo didn't know exactly where the bordello was, but he figured he could find it. He would just ask the first hardcase he saw.

Only there weren't any on Helldorado's main street this early. As Fargo looked at the men moving along the boardwalks and loading supplies into wagons in front of the general stores and the clerks helping them, he realized he was looking at the settlement's law-abiding citizens, along with sodbusters who had farms in the surrounding area. The outlaws and drifters who provided most of Helldorado's income were all denned up like wild animals this early in the day, so the normal folks thought it was safe to come out. To his surprise, Fargo even saw a few sun-bonneted women; farmers' wives, he assumed.

He stopped, leaned on one of the hitch rails, and frowned in thought. He wasn't sure he had ever come across a place like Helldorado before, a settlement that seemed to have two separate and distinct groups of inhabitants who didn't associate with each other. Ebeneezer Bates might have founded the town as a haven for men on the dodge, but given a chance Helldorado might grow and evolve into something more than that. In time it might even become a real community.

But not as long as its leading citizens were men like Bates and Donohue.

Fargo straightened. He reminded himself that he hadn't come here to solve Helldorado's ills. He was on the trail of those stolen army rifles, pure and simple. Everything else was just a distraction.

But if in finding those guns he broke up Donohue's gang and gave Helldorado a toehold on respectability, that would be an added benefit.

Fargo headed for the bordello Bates had mentioned,

hoping to find Donohue there. After asking around a bit, it was easy enough to find. It was a good-sized structure, its front wall made of weathered, unpainted planks, its sides of blocks of sod. Fargo tried the heavy door and found it unlocked. He went in, wrinkling his nose a little at the thick smell of urine, vomit, stale whiskey, and unwashed human flesh.

The door opened into a small room with a makeshift bar along the left side. Planks were laid across whiskey barrels, and a heavyset woman with iron-gray hair pulled back in a severe bun leaned on the planks. She blinked owlishly at Fargo through rimless spectacles that perched on the end of her bulbous nose. After a second, Fargo realized that she was drunk.

"Lookin' for a good time, sonny?" the woman asked. "Miss Maudie's has got the best-lookin' gals in the whole damned Nebrasky Territory."

Fargo shook his head. "I'm looking for Patch Donohue."

"Patch is a handsome man, but wouldn't you rather have a gal?"

Fargo gritted his teeth for a second as he reined in his impatience. Making his voice hard, he asked, "Where's Donohue?"

Even in her drunken stupor, the woman realized she was treading on thin ice. She put her hands on the planks and pushed herself up. Lifting her arm, she pointed a trembling finger at a door on the other side of the room. "Go down that hall. Third door on the left. But after Patch kills you for botherin' him, I'm goin' to tell him that you pulled a gun on me and made me say where he was."

Fargo smiled. "You do that."

He turned and went to the door, casting a glance over his shoulder as he did so to make sure the old woman didn't pull a gun from under the bar. She didn't. She was already slumped forward again, leaning heavily on the planks as she tried not to pass out from all the rotgut she had poured down her throat.

Shaking his head, Fargo went into the hallway beyond the door. The floor was hard-packed dirt; the walls were of sod. The doors into the tiny rooms where the girls plied their trade were nothing more than ragged sheets of canvas. Fargo paused in front of the third one on the left. He put his hand on the butt of the Colt and said, "Donohue? You in there?" Then he took a step to the right, putting himself out of the line of fire in case the outlaw decided to blast a few shots through the canvas curtain.

Instead of gunfire, Fargo heard a low, deep rumble, sort of like a bear stirring in its den, and he was reminded of what Bates had said about poking a grizzly with a stick. He said again, more sharply this time, "Donohue."

"What the hell is it? Who's out there, damn it?"

"Fargo."

A moment of silence passed, then Donohue said, "Why the hell didn't you say so? Come on in."

Cautiously, Fargo pushed the canvas flap aside and stepped into the room. There was no window. The only light came from a candle guttering on a small table beside the bunk. Donohue was lying naked on the bunk with naked young women on either side of him. His arms were flung around their shoulders, but in his right hand he held a revolver with the barrel pointing in the general direction of the door. The girl on that side, who was skinny, blond, and badly pockmarked, looked scared to death. She kept cutting her eyes toward the gun that was looming over her right shoulder.

"No need for the hogleg," Fargo said. "I'm just here to tell you that I've decided to take you up on your offer."

"You ain't worried about how the other boys'll feel, you takin' Kinnard's place like that?"

Fargo smiled contemptuously. "I'm not worried."

"Good. Anybody gives you any grief about it, you got my permission to kill 'em."

"I don't think it'll come to that."

"No, prob'ly not," Donohue agreed. "Loyalty ain't

never meant as much to the boys as money, and never will." He let the gun sag a little. "I'll be ridin' out this afternoon. Be ready to go with me."

Fargo gave a curt nod, not agreeing so much as just bringing the meeting to an end. He turned toward the door, only to stop when Donohue said his name again.

"What is it?" Fargo asked.

Donohue leered at him. The outlaw chieftain poked the barrel of the gun in his hand against the soft flesh of the blond girl's breast and used the muzzle to toy with her nipple. "You want to join me and the gals for a spell, sort of celebrate you comin' into the gang?"

Fargo felt a twinge of sickness deep inside himself at the very thought. But he managed to keep a cold expression on his face as he shook his head and said, "Thanks, but no thanks. I've got to go tend to my horse."

"Maybe another time."

"Sure," Fargo said. "Another time."

Just about the same time that a blue norther swept down on Hades and made the Devil reach for a coat, he thought.

10

With some time on his hands, Fargo went back to where the Ovaro was tied to the hitch rail. On his way up the street, he managed to look behind him a couple of times without appearing to do so. The first time he didn't see anything suspicious, but on the second occasion he caught a glimpse of what he thought was the same person he had seen the night before. The fella was loitering near one of the wagons parked in front of a store, using the vehicle to shield him as he trailed Fargo.

The Trailsman being trailed . . . Fargo grinned to himself. This wasn't the first time such a thing had happened and probably wouldn't be the last. As usual, though, he was well aware of the follower.

He was going to be patient . . . for now. It had been his experience that the best way to catch somebody was to give them plenty of chances to make a mistake. It would happen sooner or later.

Fargo untied the Ovaro and led it down the street to the emporium. Fifteen minutes later, he was cinching a new saddle in place on the big black-and-white stallion. It wasn't quite as good as his old saddle, but it would do. Once he had it broken in, it would be fine.

A short while later, Fargo found Patch Donohue in Bates's saloon, fully dressed now. Donohue tossed back the drink he was holding, made a face, wiped the back of his other hand across his mouth, and belched. "You ready to ride?" he asked Fargo.

"Just about," Fargo said. "Let me get the rest of my gear."

He fetched his rifle and saddlebags from the room where he had spent the night, and as he came downstairs, Ebeneezer Bates emerged from the office.

"What do I owe you for putting me up for the night?" Fargo asked.

Bates waved a hand. "Nothin'."

Fargo frowned and said, "You've already bought me drinks and breakfast . . ."

"Don't get the wrong idea. I'm still just as much of a mercenary son of a bitch as I ever was," Bates said with a grin. "But your bill's already paid. Donohue took care of it. He said since it was Kinnard who was to blame for puttin' you out of the loft in the livery stable, he ought to pay your room an' board."

"Did he pay Hank Jessup for the loss of the stable?"

Bates's grin became more wolfish. "I learned a long time ago not to expect miracles, Fargo."

"That's what I thought."

It didn't matter, Fargo told himself. The old man was leaving Helldorado and going to Omaha. Hank could say so long to Helldorado, and good riddance.

Donohue sauntered out of the saloon. Fargo started to follow him. Bates called out behind him, "See you around!"

Fargo waved a hand in farewell.

Outside, he saw Donohue untying the reins of a chest-nut gelding. Fargo went to the Ovaro, slung the saddle-bags over the horse's back, and strapped the sheathed Henry to the saddle. Donohue looked over at him and the stallion and said, "That's a mighty fine lookin' mount, Fargo. If you ever want to sell him, I'd be of a mind to buy."

Fargo shook his head. "He's not for sale."

Donohue gave a harsh laugh and said, "Everything's for sale. Somebody's just got to meet the price."

Not everything, Fargo thought. But he didn't bother explaining that to Donohue. Chances were, the outlaw wouldn't understand.

They rode south out of Helldorado. As Fargo looked out across the prairie in front of them, he pondered what was out there. Not much, he thought, just flat grassland cut by the Little Blue River and a few creeks, otherwise nothing until a range of small hills along the border between Nebraska Territory and Kansas. He didn't know if they would be going that far.

Fargo glanced over his shoulder. Donohue noticed and said, "Somebody on your back trail you ain't told me about, Fargo?"

"Nope. I'm just in the habit of watching it."

Donohue grunted. "That's a good habit to get into, I reckon. Helps keep a fella alive."

Fargo was looking for whoever had followed him from Omaha. The little gent would have a hard time keeping up the pursuit now. Sneaking around was almost impossible on the open prairie. There weren't enough places to hide. Maybe he should have tried to find out who the follower was, back there in Helldorado, he told himself.

Fargo wasn't one to dwell on such things, though. He dealt with matters as they were, not how they could have or should have been. He turned his attention back to the plains in front of him and Donohue.

Donohue started talking about the things he had done with the two whores at Miss Maudie's place. Fargo didn't really want to listen to the filthy stories, but he forced himself to act like he was paying attention. He was glad, though, when Donohue chuckled and admitted, "Hell, I was so drunk I don't even recollect half of the stuff we did. But I'll bet I had myself a mighty fine time."

"I'm sure you did," Fargo agreed. "You get into Helldorado often?"

"Often enough. I ain't much on towns. I like to go in ever' once in a while, get good and drunk, bed a few calico cats, maybe play some cards. I got better things to do than hang around a town, though, even one as wide open as Helldorado."

"That's the way Bates wants it, isn't it? Wide open?"

"Damn right. As soon as he started up the place, he put out the word that there wouldn't ever be no law there and hombres on the dodge were welcome. Of course, the army rides through ever' once in a while. Ain't nothin' Bates can do about that." Donohue snorted in derision. "But I ain't scared of the army. They can't do nothin' to me. They got enough to worry about, what with the Pawnee and Cheyenne and Arapaho all still on the prod over west of here."

"And all of that with them missing those rifles that were on their way to Fort Laramie." It was a risk bringing up the guns so soon, Fargo knew, but he was willing to take it. After all, the raid on the supply train was common knowledge around here. It might seem more odd if he acted like he didn't know anything about it.

Donohue gave him a sly grin. "Yeah, that was a mighty slick job, wasn't it?"

"They're still talking about it all over Omaha."

"I should hope so. Nobody's ever made off with that many army rifles at one time before." Donohue's voice was full of pride.

Fargo thought he could risk pushing just a little more. "You sound almost like you and your boys might have had something to do with it."

"Do I, now? Well, I ain't sayin' we did . . . and I ain't sayin' we didn't." The outlaw's tone hardened a little. "I ain't sayin' much of anything, Fargo, until I know for sure that I can trust you."

"Reckon only time will tell you that," Fargo said lightly.

"Yeah," Donohue said, squinting his good eye. "Time."

They rode on. Once, Fargo thought he saw another man on horseback far to the east, but that could have been anybody. Other than that, they seemed to have the prairie to themselves.

They rode on until Donohue suggested that they make camp. Fargo agreed, and a short time later they found a suitable spot in an old buffalo wallow. It hadn't rained in long enough that the ground was dry, and there were plenty of chips around for a fire. The buffalo droppings would burn with small flames and hardly any smoke, and since they were camping in a depression, the fire wouldn't be visible from the surrounding prairie. Fargo had to give Donohue credit. The outlaw knew what he was doing.

Donohue took out a frying pan and sliced thick strips off a side of bacon he took from his saddlebags. While the bacon was cooking, he mixed some biscuit dough. Fargo watched the outlaw's hands and saw that they moved smoothly and deftly. He wouldn't have figured that Donohue was much of a cook, but he knew that life on the frontier forced men to develop talents they might otherwise have never known they had. Donohue took some apples from a pouch, peeled and sliced them with his Bowie knife, and folded the sliced apples into the pockets of dough that he had formed. He grinned across the little fire at Fargo. "You're in for some good eatin'," the outlaw said.

"Looks like it," Fargo agreed. "I reckon good grub is just one of the advantages of riding with you."

"Damn right. Play square, hold up your end, and there'll be plenty of money. Not when we make the divvy from jobs we've already pulled, mind you. You got to earn your payoff."

"Like the money from those rifles?" Fargo ventured.

"Yeah," Donohue grunted. He was using the tip of his knife to flip the strips of bacon in the frying pan. He moved them around, making room for the apple-laced biscuits.

The brief exchange actually told Fargo quite a bit. For the first time, Donohue had come close to admitting that he and his men were responsible for the deadly raid on the army supply wagons. Fargo had been assuming that anyway, but it was nice to have it confirmed. Also, Donohue's comments seemed to indicate that the gang had not yet split up the profits from the sale of the rifles. That meant there was a good chance they hadn't received the payoff, and since Fargo didn't believe Donohue would let the guns out of his hands until he had the money in return for them, it was likely that the stolen rifles were still stashed somewhere, waiting for a buyer.

Fargo couldn't know that for sure, but it seemed very probable to him. So far, so good, he thought.

Donohue put coffee on to boil, and the meal was complete. When the food was ready, Fargo and Donohue dug in. The bacon was good, and Fargo had to admit that the little apple fritters were delicious.

When he was drinking a cup of coffee after the meal, Fargo asked, "Will we get to the hideout tomorrow?"

"We'll get there when we get there," Donohue said, becoming cautious again after his momentary lapse earlier.

Fargo nodded. "Sure."

Donohue looked over the lip of his cup at Fargo. "You know, there's somethin' familiar about you."

"I've been around," Fargo said casually. "Maybe you saw me somewhere."

The outlaw shook his head. "No, that ain't it. Leastways, I don't think so. Seems like I ought to recognize your name."

Fargo tried not to show how he tensed inside. He was used to people remembering the name Skye Fargo and connecting it with the even more famous nickname he bore. But the West was a mighty big place, and it didn't make sense that everybody he ran into would recognize his name. There had to be plenty of people on the frontier who didn't know Skye Fargo from Adam.

He smiled faintly, pretending to be relaxed. "Like I said, I've been around."

Donohue shrugged and said, "I reckon it ain't important, otherwise it would've come to me. Maybe it still will."

"Sure," Fargo said with a nod. That was actually the last thing he wanted, however.

Donohue finished off his coffee, then stretched his arms and gave a huge yawn. "I'm mighty tired. I'll be turnin' in. You stand the first watch, Fargo?"

"All right," Fargo said.

He got his Henry from the saddle sheath while Donohue rolled up in a blanket and stretched out on the other side of the fire. Fargo remained on his feet. He planned to walk around the camp from time to time. Looking and listening were the two main weapons a man had in the effort not to be taken by surprise. Most of the time out here, a surprised man was a dead man.

Donohue hadn't even had time to start snoring before Fargo's keen ears picked up the sound of horses approaching the buffalo wallow. Fargo dropped to his knees and hissed, "Donohue!" He crawled to the lip of the depression, facing toward the sound of the hoofbeats, and poked the barrel of his rifle out of the wallow. His eyes searched the night for any sign of the riders. From the sound of the horses, they were moving at a slow walk. The riders—three of them, Fargo judged—weren't in any hurry.

On hands and knees, Donohue moved up beside Fargo. He held a long-barreled revolver in his right hand. "What is it?" he whispered. "You hear somethin'?"

"Horses," Fargo said. "Out there."

Before Donohue had a chance to respond, a voice called out through the darkness. "Hello, the camp! We're comin' in, boss!"

Fargo shot a glance over at Donohue. "Boss?" he repeated. "You know those hombres?"

"Take it easy, Fargo," Donohue said, his voice relaxed now. "Those are two of my boys."

"Two?" Fargo said. "I hear three horses."

In the faint light of the stars, Fargo saw Donohue frown. "Yeah, you might be right," the outlaw said after a second. "Somebody must be with 'em."

For the moment, Fargo left unasked the question of why two members of Donohue's gang were wandering around the prairie in the dark. The most likely explanation was that the men had been bird-dogging them, keeping an eye on Fargo and Donohue from a distance. Fargo recalled seeing a far-off rider earlier in the day. It was possible that the men's job was to keep Donohue safe while he was traveling back and forth between Helldorado and the gang's hideout.

Those thoughts went through Fargo's brain in a flash, then he put them aside. Right now, he had to concentrate on what was happening here at the buffalo wallow. It was possible somebody had jumped Donohue's outriders. The man who had called to them might be the only one left alive, and he could have been forced to sing out like that so that Donohue wouldn't be suspicious of the approach.

"Keep your eyes open," Donohue said. "I don't much like this."

Neither did Fargo. But a moment later, as three horses loomed up out of the shadows, the man who had spoken earlier said, "Don't get trigger-happy, boss. It's just me and Hector. We got a prisoner."

That explained the third horse. Fargo could see it now. At first glance, it could have been mistaken as a pack horse, because it was carrying some sort of burden draped over its saddle. That burden, Fargo realized, was a human being, either unconscious or dead.

Donohue raised up higher. "Come on in, Buell!" he called.

Fargo and Donohue got to their feet and went back to the fire as the riders came into the buffalo wallow. Fargo watched the two men closely as they rode down the slope. The one on the left led the third horse. The fire hadn't cast much light to start with, and now that it had died down some, the glow from it was faint. The newcomers rode nearly all the way to the bottom of the depression before Fargo could get a good look at them.

When he did, he saw that they were typical hardcases, stamped with the brutality and violence of the frontier. "Howdy, boss," the one called Buell said as he dismounted. He was tall, gaunt, and hawk-faced. The other one—Hector, Buell had called him—was shorter and stockier and looked a little like a farmer in overalls and a felt hat with a ragged brim. He was the one leading the third horse. He handed the reins to Buell before swinging down from the saddle.

"Who's that?" Donohue asked, gesturing with his revolver toward the unconscious form on the third horse.

"Don't know," Buell replied, "but he was sneakin' up

on your camp when we snuck up behind him. I tapped him on the head with a gun butt while Hector caught his horse. Figured we'd better bring him on in." Buell looked at Fargo. "This the fella who killed Kinnard?"

Donohue said, "Yep," and for a second Fargo thought he might have walked into a trap. Maybe Donohue's offer of a job had been just a ruse to get him out here away from town so that the other members of the gang could take their revenge on him for Kinnard's death. But almost as soon as the idea occurred to him, he discarded it. If all Donohue and the others wanted to do was kill him, they could have done that more easily in Helldorado. Bates wouldn't have cared, and no one else in the settlement would have dared to oppose anything the outlaws wanted to do.

Buell faced Fargo, looked him up and down. Fargo met the gunman's expressionless stare with one of his own. Finally, Buell gave an ugly grin and said, "Kinnard was a good man to have on your side in a fight, but other than that, he was a mean, stupid son of a bitch. From what I hear, you didn't have any choice but to kill him."

"That's the way it appeared to me," Fargo said.

Buell shrugged. "Can't hold that against a fella." He turned to his companion. "Hector, get that yahoo down off that horse."

"Yeah," Donohue said. "I want to have a look at him."

So did Fargo. He had a hunch the prisoner was the same person who had followed him from Omaha. He had halfway expected the pursuit to continue when he and Donohue left Helldorado, and it didn't surprise him that the man had gotten himself caught.

Hector grunted, went to the third horse, and used a knife he took from under his overalls to slash the ties that held the unconscious man on the animal's back. He grabbed the man's shirt to keep him from falling, put the knife away, and then got his shoulder under the limp shape, sliding it off the horse. As he turned back toward the fire, Hector grunted again and a look of surprise appeared on his broad, dull-witted face. "This ain't right," he announced.

"What ain't right?" Donohue demanded sharply.

"I never noticed when I picked him up before . . . he ain't a him."

Hector stepped up next to the fire and dumped the captive on the ground beside the burning buffalo chips. Buell let out a whistle, and Donohue said, "Well, I'll be damned."

Fargo just stood there, staring down at the pale, dirt-streaked face of a young woman he had never seen before.

11

Her fair hair was cropped very short. She wore a man's work shirt, canvas trousers, and work boots that laced up. She had a small bruise on her cheek, probably from where she had fallen after being knocked out by Buell. It would be easy enough at first glance to take her for a man because she was so slender and the baggy clothes she wore disguised her shape to a certain extent. The way she was lying on her back, though, her breasts made unmistakable twin mounds as they pushed up against the shirt.

Hector commented on that, saying, "When I picked her up the first time and slung her on the hoss, I grabbed her 'round the waist. So I didn't feel them titties 'til just now."

"Who the hell is she?" Donohue asked. The question wasn't directed at any of the other three men in particular.

"I never saw her before, Patch," Buell said. Hector just shook his head. Donohue looked at Fargo.

"I'm just as much in the dark as you are," Fargo said. "She's not with me, that's for sure."

In truth, though, she was—in a way. He thought he recognized the canvas trousers. Put an old coat and a floppy-brimmed hat on this woman, and she would look just like the mysterious rider who had trailed him from Omaha. Without trying to be too obvious about it, Fargo took a look at the horse Hector had led into camp. It looked like the same horse his pursuer had ridden, Fargo decided. He was convinced that the young woman was the one who had followed him.

But that still didn't explain who she was or what she was doing here.

Suddenly, she let out a groan and began to stir. As she rolled onto her side, Donohue pointed his gun at her. Fargo started to say something about her not being a threat, then bit back the words. The sort of man he was pretending to be wouldn't go out of his way to be chivalrous.

"Wake up, gal," Donohue said roughly. "Who are you, and what the hell are you doin' out here?"

The woman groaned again and pushed herself up on an elbow. She shook her head a little, obviously trying to clear away the cobwebs left behind by the clout on her skull, then opened her eyes and looked around the camp in confusion. Only when her eyes fell on Fargo did they widen in some sort of recognition. "You!" she gasped. "You . . . you bastard!"

Fargo's eyes narrowed. What sort of game was she playing?

Donohue looked at Fargo. "Thought you said you didn't know her." The words held a hint of accusation.

"I don't," Fargo said.

The woman finished rolling over. She pushed herself onto hands and knees, then climbed slowly and painfully to her feet. She swayed a little from side to side as she turned to face Fargo. "You don't know me?" she said. "You think you can . . . have your way with me . . . and then run off and leave me?" She took a quick, shaky step toward him, ignoring the guns of the men around her as she hooked her fingers into claws and reached for Fargo's face. "You'd leave me . . . with child?"

Her face was contorted with rage, and her fingers were coming straight at Fargo's eyes. He had to drop the Henry to grab her wrists and stop her from clawing him. "Hold on!" he exclaimed. "Damn it, I don't know what you're talking about!"

She struggled to pull free. "The hell you don't! Don't you remember Omaha? All the beautiful things we did

104

together?" Tears began to roll down her cheeks, leaving streaks in the dust that coated them. "You said you loved me!" she wailed.

Donohue burst out in a laugh. Buell was grinning, and Hector looked vaguely amused, as if he wasn't sure of what was going on but found it funny anyway. Fargo didn't think it was funny at all. He had his hands full of a sobbing, spitting wildcat who had mistaken him for somebody else.

"I reckon I can see why you didn't want to claim her, Fargo," Donohue said. "She's a real hellion."

Fargo didn't bother anymore denying that he knew her. It might be better, he thought, to play along with her. From the first second he had seen her, he had worried about how he would protect her from Donohue and the others and still maintain his pose as one of the gang. If they were convinced that she was a ladyfriend of his—and more importantly, that she was in the family way—even ruthless desperadoes such as these would leave her alone. Until he had a chance to talk with her alone, he would let Donohue, Buell, and Hector think whatever they wanted to think.

She tried to kick him in the shin. He snapped, "That's enough," and gave her a shove that sat her down hard on her backside. "Stay there and shut up!" Fargo said, pointing a finger at her.

She put her hands over her face and started to cry harder. Fargo grimaced, turned away, looked at Donohue and the other two, and shrugged.

Donohue's expression was more serious now. "Listen here, Fargo," he said. "You can't be draggin' a gal along with you, not if you're ridin' with us. You got to do somethin' about her."

"What can I do?" Fargo asked. "I sure as hell didn't tell her to follow me."

"Put her on her horse and send her back to Helldorado," Buell suggested. "She made it out here on her own; she can make it back."

"What would she do in Helldorado?"

"Miss Maudie always needs more gals."

Something inside Fargo recoiled at the idea of this young woman working in the squalid bordello. She would be far and away the most attractive one there, though.

"Or Bates might hire her," Donohue put in. "Leastways until her belly starts to swell too much."

"All right, all right," Fargo said. "Let me talk to her." As an excuse to get the woman alone and try to find out what the devil was going on here, it would do, he decided. He walked over to her and reached down to take hold of her arm. None too gently, he pulled her to her feet. "Come on."

She didn't fight him as he led her toward the edge of the buffalo wallow. In fact, she came with him meekly this time, as if she had run out of anger. When they reached the top of the slope and Fargo judged that they were out of earshot of the outlaws, he stopped and turned toward her, putting his hands firmly on her shoulders in case the others were watching. "Who are you, really?" he said in a low-pitched voice, hoping that she wasn't so delusional that she would cling to the fantasy she had spun about the two of them a few minutes earlier.

He didn't have to worry about that. She looked at him coolly in the light of the rising moon and said, "Take it easy, Mr. Fargo. I'm not pregnant, and I'm not crazy."

His jaw tightened. "You were doing a pretty good job of acting like it."

"I know. I figured that would be the best way to keep them from getting suspicious of me. *And* the best way of getting you alone so that we can talk."

She sounded a little shaken, but for the most part she seemed pretty calm and collected. She knew who he was, that much was certain. And when she had woken up surrounded by outlaws after being knocked out, she immediately had latched on to the course of action that would keep her the safest. She was quick-witted; Fargo had to give her credit for that as well.

"Who are you?" he asked again.

"My name is Cassandra Barrett. You can call me Cass."

Fargo still had his hands on her shoulders. His fingers

tightened a little. "Barrett?" he repeated. "Any relation to Colonel Barrett in Omaha?"

"He's my father."

Fargo bit back an oath. Even though she was a woman, Cassandra Barrett's life wouldn't be worth much if Donohue found out who she really was. "What are you doing out here?"

"The same thing as you—looking for those stolen rifles."

The answer took Fargo by surprise. He said, "That's why you followed me from Omaha?"

"Yes." She spoke quickly. "Listen, Mr. Fargo. My mother died three months ago."

Fargo didn't see what that had to do with anything, but he kept silent and allowed Cass to go on.

"My father doesn't think that the frontier is any place for a proper young woman, especially one without a mother, so he's planning to send me back East to live with my aunt."

"And you don't want to go," Fargo broke in, seeing where this conversation was leading.

"No, of course not! I love it out here. I . . . I thought if I could find those rifles, the colonel would see that I can take care of myself and let me stay."

A grim smile tugged at the corners of Fargo's mouth. "You call him the colonel?"

"Everybody does."

Fargo nodded. "So you followed me in hopes that I'd lead you to the rifles?"

"Yes. I heard the colonel talking about you to Jackson . . . I mean, Lieutenant Ross. He said you were some sort of famous tracker and manhunter, and you were going to help recover the rifles." She looked up at him. "I came along to help you."

Fargo didn't point out that her "help" had put him in a bad situation. He couldn't take her on to the outlaws' hideout, but he didn't want to send her back to Helldorado on her own, either. Plus there was the question of whether or not she would actually go if he sent her away. He had his doubts.

"That was one hell of a hare-brained scheme," he said, his tone blunt.

"I had to do something. I'm supposed to leave for the East next week. It was bad enough that the colonel wanted to send me away, but when Jackson said I was just a helpless female and didn't belong out here—" She stopped short, catching her breath as if she had realized that she was saying too much.

"You wanted to show that young shavetail that he's wrong about you, didn't you?" Fargo said. "Were you and Ross interested in each other?"

Cass sniffed. "I can't speak for Lieutenant Ross, but I certainly wasn't interested in him. He's the most pompous, arrogant, overbearing—"

"Can't argue with you there," Fargo drawled.

Cass drew in a deep breath. "Anyway, I was desperate. Maybe I didn't think things through as much as I should have, but surely you can understand how I felt, Mr. Fargo."

Not being a headstrong young gal, Fargo didn't understand a bit of it, but he didn't say so. Instead, he said, as gently as could manage, "You have to turn around and go back, Miss Barrett. I hate for you to have to travel by yourself, but there's no other choice. Don't go to Helldorado, though. There's nothing there for you. Head back to Omaha as fast as you can."

"But—"

Fargo tightened his grip on her shoulders again. "No buts about it."

"That man, the one with the eye patch . . . He's Patch Donohue, isn't he? I've heard about him. He's an outlaw, maybe the worst one in the territory. He stole those rifles, didn't he?"

"That's right," Fargo admitted.

"Where are they now?"

Fargo shook his head. "I don't know."

"Has he already sold them to the Indians?"

"I don't think so," Fargo said. "From something he said earlier, it didn't sound like it."

"Then we can still get them back." There was excitement in Cass's voice.

"Not we," Fargo said. "Blast it, Miss—"

"Cass," she said. "Call me Cass."

"All right." Fargo shook her a little. "Blast it, Cass, quit arguing with me about this. I can't have you tagging along—"

From the bottom of the buffalo wallow, Donohue called, "Need a hand up there, Fargo?"

"No, it's fine," Fargo replied, then turned back to Cass and lowered his voice. "If you don't do what I told you, you'll get us both killed."

She shifted her feet. "Well . . . all right. But I don't like it."

"You don't have to like it," Fargo told her.

"Before I go, though . . ." She startled him by stepping closer to him, throwing her arms around his neck, and coming up on her toes to plant her lips against his in an urgent, searching kiss.

Fargo was a little taken aback, but he responded by sliding his arms around her waist and pulling her more tightly against him. He figured she was putting on a show for the outlaws, so they might as well be convincing about it. Her mouth was hot and wet and sweet, and the slender, rounded body felt mighty good pressed up against his. When she finally broke the kiss, he whispered, "That was just for show, right?"

She seemed a little breathless. "Y-yes. Just for show."

As she slipped out of his embrace and turned away, Fargo slapped her lightly on the rump. She let out a little yelp of surprise, then flashed a quick grin at him. He stalked down the slope into the buffalo wallow, not looking back to see if she was following him.

"The lady's going back to Helldorado," he announced to Donohue, Buell, and Hector. Hector looked a little disappointed, but Donohue nodded in satisfaction. Buell's expression was as blank as ever.

"That's good," Donohue said. "I like the gals as much as anybody, but there's places where they ain't needed."

He didn't have to add that an outlaw hideout was one of those places.

Fargo heard Cass Barrett's shuffling footsteps as she came into the camp. He motioned toward her horse and said brusquely, "Mount up and get out of here. And don't start sniveling again."

She moved past him, her eyes downcast, and gave a small, humble nod. She seemed utterly cowed by him. Fargo knew it was an act, but right now it was the best thing she could do. He watched idly as she mounted the horse and picked up the reins. The heels of her work boots jabbed the animal's flanks, and the horse trotted out of the depression, heading north toward Helldorado. Fargo felt a surge of relief when she had vanished into the darkness. He would continue to worry about her, of course, but chances were she was safer out on the prairie than she would have been with Donohue and the other outlaws.

"I hope she's at Miss Maudie's next time we go to town," Hector said. "She was sure pretty. I liked her."

"After she's been at Maudie's for a while, she won't be so pretty," Buell said. "Beauty is fleeting, especially in such surroundings."

Fargo glanced at him. Buell was well-spoken for a gunman, but the fact that he probably had had a little education didn't make him any less dangerous. It might even mean he was more so.

Donohue stepped around the fire to confront Fargo. "Now we got to talk about somethin'," he said, his voice hard and flinty. "You lied to me."

"How do you figure that?"

Donohue inclined his head toward the spot where Cass had ridden off into the darkness. "You said you didn't know that gal."

"Well, hell," Fargo said, "I never expected to see her out here. I thought she was back in Omaha." He took a guess, based on Cass's physical appearance. "Besides, the last time I saw her, she had long blond hair down her back. At first I really didn't recognize her."

Donohue's single eye was narrow with suspicion. "You sure about that?"

"Yeah, I am," Fargo said, not giving an inch. "How would you react if some gal you'd bedded once showed up weeks later and started yelling that she was going to have a baby?"

"Well . . ." Donohue relaxed slightly. "Might throw me for a loop, too, I reckon." He nodded. "All right, Fargo. Maybe you shaded the truth a little, maybe you didn't. This time, it ain't worth killin' over. But from now on, when I ask you a question, you better give me an honest answer."

"Sure," Fargo said. "Cards on the table."

"That's right. You lie, you die. Simple enough."

Fargo couldn't argue with that.

Only in this case, he knew, the truth would get him killed a lot quicker than a lie.

Since Buell and Hector had already come in and revealed their presence, there was no point in them going back out to camp elsewhere. They unsaddled their horses, made a meal of jerky and a couple of the apple fritters that were left over from Fargo and Donohue's supper, and then turned in along with their boss. Fargo stood first watch, turning the job over to Buell around midnight. The gunman didn't say anything when he took Fargo's place.

They were all up at dawn the next morning. Donohue prepared breakfast, and when the meal was finished the four men saddled up and rode on, still following a southerly direction toward the Nebraska-Kansas border. Fargo expected they would reach the little range of hills along the border by midday.

That was bound to be where Donohue's hideout was, he told himself as he rode along with the outlaws. There was nowhere else out here on this prairie that would offer any shelter.

To pass the time, he said to Donohue, "Do you always have a couple of men watching your back when you go into town?"

"The man who stays alert is the man who stays alive," Donohue said. "Most folks out here know to steer clear of me, but there's no tellin' when you'll run into a war party or a cavalry patrol. So, yeah, I usually take a couple o' the boys with me as outriders."

"Smart," Fargo said.

"That's how I've stayed alive this long," Donohue replied with a wolfish grin. He chuckled. "That, and friends in high places."

Fargo wondered what in blazes the outlaw chief meant by that, but Donohue didn't seem inclined to elaborate and Fargo didn't think it would be wise to press the issue. They rode on.

Later, the hills came in sight, low brown humps against the southern horizon. The sun climbed toward its zenith. As Fargo expected, the hot, brassy orb was almost directly overhead when they rode into the hills. Fargo's eyes were narrowed against the glare of the light.

He didn't see the cave until they were nearly on top of it. It was set into the side of one of the hills, its mouth low, black, and uninviting. The men had to dismount and lead their horses inside.

"There used to be an old underground stream down here," Donohue said, his voice echoing from the low dirt ceiling. Fargo saw that thick timbers had been placed along the walls to hold up that ceiling. There were no trees within fifty miles big enough to have provided those heavy beams. Someone had brought them in from far away to shore up the tunnel. Fargo rested a hand on one of them for a second, able almost to feel the antiquity in it.

As if reading Fargo's mind, Buell said, "Conquistadors is my guess. Some folks say that Coronado made it this far north when he came up from Mexico looking for the seven cities of gold. And I found a knife in here once that looked Spanish. It was old, really old."

Fargo nodded. He, too, had heard stories of the Conquistadors, the Spanish explorers who had penetrated far into the North American continent in centuries past. Why they had brought logs all the way from New Mexico

Territory and used them to form support beams for this cave, that was anybody's guess. Fargo would have been willing to bet that it had something to do with the Spaniard's lust for gold, though, a lust that Coronado and those like him had never gotten over.

He saw light up ahead. The tunnel-like cave widened out into a larger room. A rope corral had been fashioned on one side, and half a dozen horses were there, making the smoky air thick with the smell of horseflesh and dung. On the other side of the chamber, a fire burned, and the men who owned the horses sat around the flames, passing a bottle back and forth. They would be the rest of the outlaw gang, Fargo knew.

All except for one, and he was just about the last person on the face of the earth that Fargo expected to see here in this den of cutthroats.

Hank Jessup lifted the bottle of whiskey in his hand in greeting and grinned. "Howdy, Mr. Fargo," he said. "I decided not to go see that colonel who's a friend of yours and take that job with the cavalry like you told me to."

12

"Hank, what the hell!" Donohue burst out.

For a second, Fargo thought that the old stablekeeper had somehow fallen in with these outlaws by accident. But then he saw the gleam of cunning in Hank Jessup's eyes and knew that it wasn't an accident at all that Jessup was here. He hadn't revealed Fargo's connection with the cavalry by accident, either.

"You're a damned fool, Patch," Jessup went on. "You might as well invite a rattlesnake into your blankets as bring the Trailsman down here to the hideout."

Donohue's head jerked around. He stared at Fargo, who stood there easily, his muscles relaxed, but ready for instant movement. Fargo's plan was shot to hell and the rest of his life might be measured out in mere minutes, but all he could do was wait and see how it would all play out.

"The Trailsman!" Donohue repeated. "That's why your name sounded so damned familiar! I knew I'd heard it before."

"You're just lucky I knew who he was," Jessup said. His words came more quickly now. The slow, querulous tone he had adopted as a liveryman in Helldorado was gone. Fargo felt a touch of annoyance at himself for letting Hank Jessup fool him like that. The old man was good, though. He was about as slick a crook as Fargo had ever come across.

And there was no doubt in Fargo's mind now that Jessup was an outlaw, too. Otherwise he wouldn't be sitting there so comfortably and talking to Donohue like he was.

Not everyone had known of Jessup's connection to the gang, however. One of the men sitting by the fire said to Donohue, "Then this old-timer was tellin' us the truth when he rode up, Patch? You and him really are partners?"

"Silent partners," Jessup put in.

"Yeah, yeah," Donohue snapped. "I figured it'd be a good idea to have somebody lookin' out for our interests in Helldorado, just in case that bastard Bates decided he'd be better off sellin' us out to the army or somethin' like that."

So Ebeneezer Bates, despite being no more honest than he had to be, wasn't tied in directly with the gang. Fargo filed away that bit of information in his brain, even though from the looks of things, he might never get the chance to make use of it. In fact, the way things stood now, he didn't have much of a chance of ever getting out of this old Spanish cave alive. He was outnumbered ten to one, and every man in here was capable of gunning him down in cold blood without blinking an eye.

Which meant he didn't have anything to lose by trying a bluff. "Bates didn't sell you out to the army," he said to Donohue, "but that doesn't mean the cavalry won't come boiling in here any minute now."

Buell stepped up behind Fargo and dug the barrel of a gun into his back. "What are you talking about?"

If Cass Barrett had ridden all night the way Fargo hoped she had, then she was well on her way back to Omaha by now. He had to assume that she'd done as he had told her, so that she would be safely out of reach of these murderers. "That girl you and Hector grabbed last night was working with me," he said. "She's gone to bring the cavalry. We worked it all out while we were talking. They've been following her ever since we left Omaha."

"She ain't a whore?" Hector said, sounding disappointed.

"Afraid not," Fargo said.

Donohue stepped in front of him, a sneer on his craggy face. "You're full o' buffalo chips, Fargo. Even if that gal really did ride off to look for the army, she don't know where we are."

"She knows the right direction, and I told her I figured the hideout was somewhere in these hills." Fargo tried to make his voice sound more confident than he felt. "They'll find it, all right, and when they do, that'll be the end for you and your gang."

Donohue drew one of his long-barreled pistols. He laid the muzzle of the gun alongside Fargo's nose. "Even if ever'thing you say is right, you won't be around to appreciate any of it, Fargo—because I'm about to put a bullet right through that lyin' head of yours."

Fargo had Donohue's gun in his face and Buell's in his back. He had no room to twist away, nowhere to run that bullets couldn't chop him down in a matter of instants. He had been in plenty of tight spots in his adventurous career, but none any tighter or deadlier than this.

Then, before either of the outlaws could pull trigger, a clatter of hoofbeats sounded outside, followed by the blowing of a bugle. Instinctively, Donohue jerked the gun away from Fargo's cheek and turned toward the tunnel that led to the surface. "Son of a bitch!" he exclaimed. "The cavalry!"

Instantly, all the outlaws were on their feet, guns drawn, ready to fight. One of them yelped, "They got us trapped like rats! Let's get outta here!"

Several of them rushed toward the entrance. Without Donohue's gun in his face anymore, Fargo had room to move. He threw himself aside even as Buell's gun blasted. The bullet plucked at the side of Fargo's buckskin shirt as he spun around. His elbow came up and back and smashed into Buell's jaw. Buell went down in a limp sprawl, out cold.

Donohue twisted back toward Fargo, trying to bring his gun to bear on the Trailsman. Fargo was already palming out his own Colt, however, and the revolver bucked against his palm as he fired from the hip. The slug sizzled past Donohue's ear, so close that the outlaw chieftain involuntarily cried out and ducked aside.

That gave Fargo the chance to step forward and slam the barrel of his gun across Donohue's face. At the same time, the side of his other hand chopped down on Donohue's gun wrist, knocking the weapon out of the outlaw's hand. Fargo grabbed the shoulder of the stunned Donohue and jerked him around. Fargo's left arm looped around Donohue's neck and clamped down tightly. He jammed the barrel of the Colt into Donohue's side.

"Everybody hold it!" Fargo shouted, his voice echoing loudly in the close confines of the cave. "Drop your guns or I'll blast Donohue's guts out!"

"Shoot him!" Donohue howled. "Forget about me! Kill the bas—"

Fargo's arm tightened even more and choked off Donohue's words. The other bandits hesitated, giving Fargo the chance to retreat a few steps and put his back against the wall of the cave. He dragged Donohue with him.

Outside, the bugle was still blowing, but the sound was fainter now, as if the bugler was riding away. Fargo hadn't heard any shots outside, either. He wasn't sure what was going on out there, but he felt confident that the cavalry hadn't ridden to his rescue. None of the soldiers had any idea where he was.

At the moment, all he cared about was continuing to postpone the doom that had looked certain only moments earlier. The other outlaws weren't shooting at him, but they weren't surrendering or dropping their guns, either. Mostly they were just standing there looking confused and unsure what to do next.

All but Hank Jessup. He had bolted to his feet with the others, but he still stood by the fire, smiling at Fargo. "That won't do you any good, Mr. Fargo," he said. "You still ain't gettin' out of here alive. Even if you pull the trigger on Patch, we'll shoot you to doll rags 'fore he hits the ground."

Fargo had hoped he could bluff his way out of here using Donohue as a human shield before that thought occurred to the other outlaws. Even if that wasn't going to work, he wasn't ready to give up.

"The cavalry—" he began.

Jessup waved a gnarled hand toward the cave mouth. "There ain't no cavalry out there. If there was, they'd have come boilin' in here by now." He raised his voice to call to the men who had rushed out. "You fellers see any cavalry out there?"

Several of the outlaws walked down the tunnel from the entrance. Hector was among them, and he said, "There ain't nobody around—" He stopped short when he saw Fargo holding Donohue hostage and Buell stretched out unconscious on the floor. "Say, what happened here?"

Jessup ignored Hector's question and said to Fargo, "I don't know how you got that bugle to blow. I'd think we just imagined it if we hadn't all heard it."

The bugle hadn't been imaginary. Fargo was sure of that. But he had no explanation for it, and the hope that it had given him was fading away rapidly. Jessup raised the pistol in his hand and went on, "You better give up now, Mr. Fargo, or things'll just get worse."

How much worse could it get, Fargo wondered. He was facing almost certain death no matter what he did.

A second later, he realized he should never tempt fate that way. He heard what sounded like a woman's voice cry out in pain, then a slap, then a man's familiar harsh voice saying, "Quit your squirmin', damn it!"

The men in the tunnel jerked around, guns rising, and the same man's voice commanded, "Put those guns down and let me through, you damned fools." The outlaws backed away from the tunnel with their guns still trained on it, and a tall, broad-shouldered, powerful figure in the uniform of a cavalry trooper strode into the cave with a struggling body flung over his shoulder. Sergeant Luther Creed glared around at the outlaws and dumped Cass Barrett at his feet. He grinned at Donohue and said, "Patch, tell your boys to take it easy. I've done pulled your fat outta the fire for you."

Fargo tried not to stare in amazement at Cass and Creed. Donohue had said that he had friends in high places; Fargo wasn't sure how high a cavalry sergeant was, but he figured Donohue had been talking about Creed. No wonder Lieutenant Ross's patrol hadn't been able to find the outlaws. Ross was green; he probably leaned heavily on his sergeant for guidance. And Creed had no doubt steered him away from Donohue's hideout any time it appeared that the patrol might accidentally stumble upon it.

Having Skye Fargo on the trail of the gang must have been one of the last things Creed wanted. But he hadn't been able to do anything about it. He could influence a young shavetail, but not an experienced officer like Colonel Thomas Barrett. He must not have had any chance to send word to Donohue, either, warning him about Fargo.

"It's that gal again," Hector said as he stared hungrily at Cass, who lay there on the floor of the cave glaring at the outlaws. "The pretty one."

"She's Colonel Barrett's daughter," Creed snapped. "I found her riding around out there and blowing on some damned bugle she got from somewhere." His gaze was fixed on Fargo and Donohue. The crooked sergeant went on, "Patch, I don't know how you got yourself into this fix unless you were dumb enough to trust Fargo here."

Donohue made a growling sound deep in his throat and tried to pull away from Fargo, only to have Fargo ram the barrel of the Colt into his side with more force. "Take it easy," Fargo said. "Nobody has to die here."

Jessup spoke up, saying, "I reckon you're right about that, Mr. Fargo. Drop that gun, and we won't kill you or the girl. Not yet, anyway."

Creed switched his stare to Jessup. "Who the hell are you, old man?"

One of the other outlaws answered, "Him and Patch are partners."

Creed looked back at Fargo and Donohue, his eyes calculating. "Is that so?" he said. "Just how many partners you got in this game, Patch?"

Donohue squirmed some more and made incoherent sounds, ignoring the warning that Fargo had given him earlier.

Given time, Fargo might have been able to use Creed's suspicion of Donohue to drive a wedge between the two men. There was no time, however. He couldn't blast away at Creed, Jessup, and the others, using Donohue as a shield as he did so, without risking Cass's life. Not that such a grandstand play would have gotten him out of here alive, he told himself. But at least he could have taken some of the bastards down with him.

"You're a smart man, Mr. Fargo," Jessup went on. "You can see you ain't got any other choice. Drop that gun, and I give you my word nobody'll get hurt."

From the floor of the cave, Cass said urgently, "Don't do it, Fargo! Don't worry about me. Just shoot Donohue and Creed and that old man!"

Jessup smiled at Fargo. "Maybe you *could* drop all three of us before we kill you and the girl," he said. "Is it worth it, Mr. Fargo?"

Fargo took a deep breath; then, seeing that he had no other choice, he pulled the gun away from Donohue's side, eased the hammer down, and let it slip to the ground with a *thud*. Without the threat of the Colt to deter him, Donohue tore free from Fargo's grasp and swung around. His fist sledged into Fargo's jaw and knocked the Trailsman back against the wall. Next Donohue buried his other first in Fargo's belly, doubling him over. Pain shot through Fargo, and every instinct in his body was screaming out for him to fight back. He kept that impulse under control, knowing that the enraged Donohue would kill him despite Jessup's promise, if given even half a chance.

Donohue clasped his hands together and clubbed them down on the back of Fargo's neck. Fargo heard Cass scream as he fell to the cave floor. Hunched up, he grunted in pain as one of Donohue's booted feet crashed into his side in a vicious kick.

"You sorry son of a bitch," Donohue grated. "I'm gonna stomp the life out of you."

"No!" Jessup said sharply. "Don't kill him. I gave my word."

Fargo twisted his head so that he could look up and see Donohue and Jessup staring hard at each other. This was a test to see who held the true power in the gang, and he had no idea who was going to prevail.

Somewhat to Fargo's surprise, it was Jessup. Donohue gave a curt nod and said, "All right. I won't kill him. But I can kick him half to death, can't I?"

Jessup grinned. "I never said you couldn't do that."

Donohue swung back toward Fargo. Fargo tried to twist out of the way, but he was already too stunned to move fast enough. Donohue kicked him again and sent him rolling against the wall. The outlaw followed, stomping and kicking, and there was nothing Fargo could do except endure the awful punishment Donohue was dishing out.

He passed out after what seemed like a long time but was probably only a few minutes. The last thing he was aware of was Cass Barrett screaming.

Consciousness returned slowly and painfully to Fargo. One thing he had learned over the years was that pain was preferable to oblivion. It meant that a man was still alive.

He kept his eyes closed for the time being as his senses awakened. He could smell smoke from the fire, hear the murmur of men's voices, and feel the rocky floor of the cave beneath his bruised, pain-wracked body. He didn't want to announce that he was conscious again, however, until he had a better idea of what was going on around him and what kind of shape he was in.

He had a hunch that the answer to the last question was "pretty bad." Carefully, he deepened his breathing, expanding his lungs and waiting for the telltale thrust of agony that would tell him he had broken ribs. When it didn't come, he knew he'd had at least a little luck on his side. Considering how brutally Donohue had attacked him, he wouldn't have been surprised if several of his ribs were broken.

But since that wasn't the case, Fargo proceeded with the inventory of damage to his body. His head hurt like someone was pounding on the inside of his skull with a sledgehammer. He could ignore that for the time being, he told himself. He tensed the muscles in his arms and legs, moving them in tiny increments, so that no one would notice the movements without looking directly at him. Again he waited for the pain of broken bones to assert itself. When it didn't come, his feeling of relief grew.

All right, he told himself. So he had taken a beating. It wasn't the first time. Probably wouldn't be the last.

The touch of something cool and soft on his forehead was so shocking that he almost jumped and yelled. He fought down the impulse, but he couldn't keep himself from opening his eyes. He found himself looking up into the tense, worried face of Cass Barrett.

She was resting her hand on his forehead. She leaned closer to him and whispered, "Skye . . ."

The look in his eyes made her fall silent. He gave a minuscule shake of his head to let her know that he didn't want the outlaws alerted that he was awake. Turning his head slightly, he peered through slitted eyes around the cave.

A dozen feet away, Donohue, Jessup, and Creed sat beside the fire talking. The other members of the gang were scattered around the chamber, some of them drinking, some of them playing cards, a couple tending to the horses in the rope corral. And one man stood by the tunnel that led to the surface, slouched against the wall, thumbs hooked in his gunbelt, but his eyes were alert. He was standing guard so that Fargo and Cass couldn't make a break for the entrance.

"—get 'em now before it's too late," Creed was saying.

"Nobody's goin' to find them rifles," Jessup replied. "They'll be safe as houses until we get word from Cut Ear to meet him and turn them over to him."

Cut Ear. Fargo recognized the name from talk he had heard along the trail while he was guiding that wagon train. Cut Ear was a young Pawnee war chief, an up-

and-coming warrior who was out to make a name for himself in the tribe by slaughtering as many of the white interlopers as he could. His raids had been fairly small so far, though deadly in their savagery. But if Cut Ear got his hands on a couple of hundred new rifles, he could inspire a much larger band of warriors to follow him, and the blood they would spill and the horror they would wreak across the prairie would be incredible.

"That's what I've been tryin' to tell you," Creed said. "I got the word from one of our scouts who's been workin' with me. Cut Ear's ready to meet. He's talked the big chiefs into turnin' over a bunch of the loot they've squirreled away from their raids over the past couple of years. The money don't mean nothin' to them, of course, but I'm glad they hung on to it. That's why I risked ridin' out here."

"Won't the army be after you for desertion now?" Jessup asked.

Creed laughed. "Once I get my share of the payoff, you reckon I'm goin' to care about a little thing like that?"

"If they're lookin' for you, they're liable to find us," Jessup complained, a cantankerous note in his voice. "I don't like it."

"Yeah, I can understand why you're so pleased with what you've been doin' so far," Creed shot back. "You let the Trailsman waltz right in here, and you even let a girl find your hideout."

"That's enough." Donohue's voice was edged with steel. "Both of you pull in your spurs. We've all made mistakes. If I'd told Kinnard you were one of us, Hank, he'd never have burned down your stable goin' after Fargo."

"That's over and done with. What's important now is gettin' that money from Cut Ear for those rifles."

Creed said, "Hadn't somebody better tell me where the guns are, just in case something happens to you, Patch?"

"I ain't the only one who knows," Donohue replied. "But nothin's goin' to happen to me before we get the guns. Sounds to me like we ought to saddle up and fetch them right now."

"That's a good idea," Jessup agreed. He turned to point toward the other side of the cave. "But what about Fargo and the girl?"

Cass's hand had dropped to Fargo's shoulder. He felt her fingers tighten as Jessup voiced the question.

"I say we hang on to the girl," Creed declared. "Just in case we run across the cavalry, they won't dare try anything if we've got the colonel's daughter. She's all Barrett's got left since her ma died, and that young idiot Ross is sweet on her."

Donohue asked, "You really think they'd let us go to save her life?"

"They wouldn't like it, but they'd do it," Creed said with confidence. "Barrett's a hard-nosed, by-the-book son of a bitch, but she's his daughter. He'd do anything to see that she's safe."

"All right, then. We don't kill the girl. What about Fargo?"

With some relish, Creed said, "Now that's a different story. I can't think of any reason to keep that bastard alive."

"Maybe you can't, but he saved my life," Jessup said. "Kinnard likely would've killed me if Fargo hadn't stopped him, and I've have burned to death for sure if he hadn't got me out of the stable. So I owe him something."

"Let it be a quick death, then, instead of a hard one," Donohue suggested. "I get the feelin' Creed here would like to see Fargo take a long time to die."

Creed grunted. "Damned straight."

For a long moment, Jessup didn't say anything. Then Fargo saw him nod slowly, and he said, "Yeah, I reckon Fargo's got to die. But let me be the one to do it."

"You can go put a bullet through his brain right now for all I care," Donohue said. He spat into the fire to emphasize his feelings.

"No, I want him to know there ain't no hard feelin's," Jessup insisted. "You fellas take the girl and go on and get those guns. I'll stay here and take care of Fargo when he wakes up."

"What?" Creed exclaimed. "That's crazy!"

"That's the way I want to do it," Jessup said. "And I'm callin' the shots around here."

Creed turned to Donohue. "Patch, do I have to listen to this old coot—"

"Yes," Donohue said heavily before the renegade sergeant could finish the question. "Hank and I been workin' together for a long time, and he ain't never steered me wrong."

Creed sneered. "Are you sayin' that some addlepated old-timer is the brains o' this operation?"

Jessup moved with the speed of a striking snake. He had his pistol out and the barrel pressed against Creed's nose before the big noncom could blink. "You're forgettin' that we don't really need you no more," Jessup said in a hissing voice.

Creed sat there as still as a stone. He swallowed once, but that was the only move he made as he stared cross-eyed at the barrel of the gun just below his eyes. Finally he croaked, "The hell you don't need me. I know where we're supposed to meet Cut Ear with those guns. None of you do."

"He's right, Hank," Donohue said. "Put the gun away. We got to get along if we want that payoff."

The group of outlaws playing cards hadn't stopped their game when Jessup pulled his gun. Buell was among them, and he said now, "Patch Donohue, the voice of reason. Who would have thought it?"

"Shut up, Buell," Donohue said easily. "Just 'cause you got more schoolin' than the rest of us don't give you leave to run off at the mouth."

"Sorry, boss," Buell said, though he didn't sound very repentant to Fargo. The hawk-faced gunman went back to his card playing.

"All right, then, it's settled," Donohue said. "Hank, you'll stay here and get rid of Fargo. The rest of us will take the girl and go get the rifles, and Creed will lead us to Cut Ear."

"That's it," Creed said. "Are you goin' to catch up to us, old man?"

Jessup shook his head. "Nope, I reckon I'll just mosey back in to Helldorado after you're gone. Nobody there knows I'm tied up with you boys. I'll use my share of the money to rebuild the stable and go back to scoutin' out good jobs for Patch here to pull."

"It'll take us the rest of the night and all day tomorrow to get to Helldorado," Donohue said. "We'll get the guns tomorrow night. You can drift back in day after tomorrow, Hank."

"Yep. Sounds good."

So the stolen rifles were in Helldorado, Fargo thought. The information might not do him any good, but at least he knew now where to find them if he got the chance. He wasn't going to give up yet. Not while there was still breath in his body.

Donohue came to his feet and turned to call, "Saddle up, boys. We'll be ridin' in a few minutes."

Fargo caught Cass's eye and mouthed "Don't worry" at her. He hoped it wasn't hollow encouragement. He was banking on being able to get away from Hank Jessup once the other outlaws were gone. It was a slim chance, considering the shape he was in, but any chance was better than none.

Then he closed his eyes as Creed stood up and turned toward them. He heard the sergeant stalk across the room, and then Cass let out a little cry. Fargo figured Creed had grabbed her arm and jerked her to her feet. "Come on, little miss," Creed said. "You're goin' with me."

"My father's going to kill you," Cass said in a low, intense voice filled with hatred.

Creed just laughed. "Not likely. Not as long as I got you."

Fargo was counting on that, too. He didn't want the outlaws to get into a pitched battle with the cavalry until he'd had an opportunity to get Cass away from them. Everything would have to break just right for that to happen . . .

The next few minutes were busy ones, as the members of the gang saddled their horses and got ready to leave the hideout. Fargo continued to feign unconsciousness. He wasn't sure how long he could pull that off, but for him and Cass to have any chance of coming through this alive, the pose had to be successful until Donohue and the others were gone, leaving him alone with Jessup.

With a great clatter of hoofbeats that echoed against the low ceiling, the outlaws rode out of the cave. "See you around, Hank!" Donohue called.

"You better!" Jessup replied. "And you better have my share of the loot when you do!"

Donohue just laughed as he followed the other outlaws into the tunnel.

Fargo didn't budge. He still lay as he had the entire time, his eyes closed, his breathing regular, apparently out cold. To maintain that attitude required quite an effort of will, but he called on his reserves of strength to do so. Finally, the sounds of the horses faded away completely, and the cave was silent except for the faint crackling of the fire.

Then Fargo heard feet shuffling across the ground as Hank Jessup approached him. "I sure wish things had turned out different, Mr. Fargo," Jessup said, addressing him as if Fargo were awake. Fargo was, of course, but Jessup didn't know that. "I knew you was the one they call the Trailsman right off, but I was hopin' that you weren't workin' for the army. Once you said that about Colonel Barrett, though, I knew it would come down to this sooner or later. But I really am sorry I got to do it."

A second later, Fargo heard a sound that he recognized all too well, a sound he had heard many times before in his life.

The unmistakable metallic ratcheting of a revolver's hammer being drawn back to full cock . . .

13

Fargo couldn't help it. Even his iron will was not powerful enough to keep his eyes from snapping open. He knew that Jessup had said he was going to wait until Fargo was awake to kill him, but that was no guarantee the old man actually would do so.

Jessup chuckled as he saw Fargo staring up at him. "I thought you might be awake," he said. "Figured the sound of a gun bein' cocked would make you open your eyes if you was. How much did you hear?"

"Enough to know you're . . . a sidewinder and a polecat," Fargo rasped out. His voice sounded harsh to his ears, like the squeal of rusty hinges. He tasted blood in his mouth and turned his head to spit.

That brought a laugh from Jessup. "You still got spirit. I figured Donohue could stomp you from here to Sunday, but he wouldn't never break you. That's why I got to kill you." Jessup hunkered on his haunches, which brought him a little closer to Fargo, but he was still out of reach. "If I let you live, you'd never rest until you'd tracked down all of us, would you?"

"Not likely," Fargo said. There was no point in lying.

"I'll make it quick, like I promised. 'Fore I do that, though, there's a few things I want to know. How'd that little gal get mixed up in this?"

Fargo didn't see any reason to lie about what Cass had told him. And the longer he kept Jessup talking, the more time he had for some of his strength to return to him.

"Her father is sending her back East to live with relatives, and she doesn't want to go. She got the idea in her head that if she found those stolen rifles, the colonel would let her stay out here. She was trying to impress a young lieutenant as well."

"That was a mighty foolish thing for her to do."

Fargo nodded. "Yes, but when you're young, sometimes you don't think things through all the way. Hell, even old people make mistakes."

"We sure do," Jessup said. "One of mine was putting too much trust in that lunkhead nephew of mine."

"Donohue's your nephew?" The question was startled out of Fargo.

"That's right. And he didn't even think to post a guard outside the cave after he got back with you and the others. That's how come the girl was able to sneak up and hear what was goin' on in here. That tunnel carried our voices right outside. She'd brought a cavalry bugle with her from Omaha, sort of a good luck piece, she said, so she started racin' around and tootin' on it hopin' to draw us out of here so you could get away. It was her bad luck that Creed came ridin' up right then."

"You questioned her after Donohue knocked me out?"

"Yeah, but nobody hurt her," Jessup said. "I wouldn't stand for that, and Patch knows to go along with what I say. Shoot, that boy couldn't find his own ass in a wash bucket if he didn't have me around to help him out."

"So you think Cass Barrett is safe," Fargo said, bitter anger edging into his voice. "Don't you know what'll happen to her as soon as Donohue and Creed don't have any use for her anymore?"

"Whatever happens then, it ain't my look-out," Jessup said. "Maybe they'll send her back to her pa. It could happen." The old man rubbed his lean, stubbly jaw. "On the other hand, Cut Ear might pay even more to have the daughter of a bluecoat chief turned over to him . . ."

That was what Fargo had been thinking. If he didn't catch up to Donohue and Creed before their meeting with the Pawnee war chief, Cass's chances for survival were very slender indeed.

Jessup gestured with the barrel of the gun he held. "The other thing I want to know is, do you have any idea where them guns are now?"

"Why do you want to know?" Fargo shot back. "Just so you can gloat over how smart you are?"

"No, I figured if you didn't know, that meant the hidin' place was a good 'un, good enough to use again, maybe."

Fargo shook his head, ignoring the extra hammering that set off inside his skull. "No, I don't know," he admitted.

Jessup cackled with laughter. "You done walked right over 'em more'n once. The crates are buried under my stable in Helldorado."

"The stable burned down."

"Didn't hurt them guns. They're buried deep enough so's the fire never touched 'em. All Patch and his boys have to do is move some of the debris aside and dig 'em up. Then they can head for that rendezvous with Cut Ear."

"You and Donohue were the only ones who knew that?"

"Yep. It was mighty hard work, buryin' the crates like that by ourselves, but we managed. Like you said yourself, Mr. Fargo, I'm a hard worker even if I am an old man."

"Why'd you wait until this late in your life to turn crooked?"

"Who says I did?" Jessup let out another cackle of laughter. "Shoot, twenty or thirty years ago, I slit more throats on the Natchez Trace than anybody you ever saw. Me an' my sis—Patch's ma—worked the riverboats, too." A wistful look came into Jessup's eyes. "Them was mighty good days. I sure do miss 'em sometimes."

Fargo repressed a shudder at the note of nostalgia in Jessup's voice as the old man recalled what must have been a lifetime of murder and crime. He had no doubt now that Jessup was the real ringleader of the gang, pulling the strings behind the scenes with no one the wiser—until now.

"All right, I reckon that about does it," Jessup went

on, coming back from his brief reverie with a little shake of his head. "We done enough palaverin'. I got to plug you now, Fargo, and then I'll start back to Helldorado in the mornin'." He lifted the gun. "You want to close your eyes, or you want to watch the bullet comin'?"

"I'd rather you give me a chance to fight."

"Do I look like a fool? I know I couldn't take you, boy, even after you've had the hell stomped out of you. No, that's it. Sorry."

For the past few minutes, Fargo had been working the toe of his boot behind one of the small rocks that littered the floor of the cave. He had no weapons, and he wasn't foolish enough to think that he could accomplish anything with a rock.

Except maybe a distraction. Right now, that was the best he could hope for.

With a convulsive movement of his leg, he kicked the rock toward Jessup. It didn't come that close to the old man, but close enough so that he saw it from the corner of his eye and jerked the muzzle of the gun a fraction of an inch in that direction. The pistol cracked wickedly, but Fargo was moving even as Jessup fired. The bullet came so close that Fargo felt it burn the lobe of his right ear before it smacked into the wall behind him. He flung himself across the distance between himself and Jessup, ignoring the screams from his pain-wracked muscles.

Jessup's gun blasted again, the echoes of the report deafening as they rebounded from the walls and ceiling of the cave. Fargo didn't know if he was hit or not. His diving tackle smashed into Jessup and took the old man down. Jessup cried out as he crashed to the ground with Fargo on top of him.

Fargo's left hand found the wrist of Jessup's gun hand and twisted hard. Jessup yelped again. Fargo's right fist cracked against Jessup's jaw. The blow drove Jessup's head against the ground. The elderly killer went limp.

Fargo had to rein in the impulse to hit Jessup again and again until the old man was dead. With an effort, Fargo forced himself to get to his feet. He picked up Jessup's gun and put it in his own empty holster. Jessup's breathing was ragged, and his eyes were rolled up in their sockets. He wouldn't come to for at least several minutes, Fargo judged.

Fargo used a couple of those minutes to stand there with one hand braced against the wall for support and regain some more strength. The fight with Jessup, brief though it had been, had taken a lot out of him in his current condition. But after a few moments he began to feel better, and the pain in his head subsided a little. He was able to bend over, yank Jessup's belt out of the loops on his trousers, and use the belt to tie the old man's hands behind his back.

One thing Fargo had noticed earlier was that the Ovaro was not inside the cave with the other horses. Probably what had happened was that one of the outlaws had tried to grab the stallion's reins after Fargo was knocked out, and the Ovaro had shied away and run out of the cave. No one could catch the big black-and-white horse if it didn't want to be caught. If Fargo's hunch was right, the stallion would be waiting somewhere close by on the prairie, listening for its master's call.

Jessup's horse was still there, tied to an outcropping of rock. The animal was nervous, spooked by the loud gunfire and the smell of powder smoke. As Fargo approached, the horse danced around skittishly. It took Fargo several minutes of talking in a low, calm voice before the horse began to settle down. When he had the animal under control, Fargo untied the reins and led it up the tunnel to the surface, emerging on the side of the hill.

Night had fallen while Fargo was unconscious. A look at the stars told him that it had been dark for several hours. The moon was already rising as well.

Holding on to the reins of Jessup's horse, Fargo let out a low, piercing whistle. There was no response, so he tried again. This time he heard hoofbeats approaching, and a couple of seconds later, the stallion trotted up out of the darkness. Fargo heaved a sigh of relief. He had seldom been so glad to see anybody or anything.

His Henry rifle was still in the saddle boot. Jessup's

revolver was a Colt, the same caliber as the one Fargo normally carried, though a slightly older model. He had plenty of ammunition for both weapons. His Arkansas toothpick was gone, probably claimed by one of the outlaws. Maybe he would get it back when he caught up with the gang.

He tied the second horse to a small greasewood bush but didn't bother with the Ovaro. Now that he had called the stallion to him, it wasn't going anywhere. Fargo went back down the tunnel to the cave. Jessup had regained consciousness by now, and he glared ferociously at Fargo as the Trailsman entered the underground chamber.

"I'll skin you alive, boy!" the old man threatened. "I'm gonna make you wish you'd never been born! Time I get through with you, you'll be beggin' for a bullet—"

Fargo bent down, yanked Jessup's bandanna from around the scrawny neck, and jammed the cloth into Jessup's mouth. "Shut up," Fargo said. "I'm tired of listening to you, old man."

He took hold of Jessup's legs and started dragging him out of the cave. Jessup squirmed and twisted and made furious but incoherent noises as he tried unsuccessfully to spit out the gag. Fargo didn't worry too much about being gentle as he hauled Jessup outside, picked him up, and lifted him onto the second horse. Jessup was so skinny that hefting him was like lifting a bundle of knobby sticks covered in old leather.

Fargo tied Jessup into the saddle, lashing his feet together under the horse's belly. Jessup was still making noises. "Might as well shut up," Fargo told him. "If you don't, I'll tie that gag in place, and it'll be even more uncomfortable."

Jessup still grumbled incomprehensibly for a moment, but his protests gradually subsided. Fargo jerked the horse's reins loose from the bush and held them as he swung up into the saddle on the back of the Ovaro. He heeled the stallion into a trot, heading north toward Helldorado, leading the other horse. There was plenty of light from the moon and stars. Fargo knew he would have little trouble retracing the path that had brought him to the isolated cave that had served as Donohue's hideout.

The outlaws wouldn't be returning here. Fargo intended to see to that. Unknown to Donohue and his cohorts, all they had waiting for them in the future was a prison cell and most likely the gallows. Or a coffin and a lonely grave even sooner, if that was the way they wanted it.

After all Fargo had been through, he didn't really care. Either way was fine with him.

Fargo still had jerky in his saddlebags. He and Jessup breakfasted on strips of it at dawn the next morning when Fargo called a halt to rest the horses. When Fargo removed the gag, Jessup begged to have his hands untied, but Fargo refused. He said, "Open wide," and stuck a piece of jerky in the old man's mouth. "You can manage just fine with that."

Jessup gnawed on the dried, smoked meat until it had softened up enough that he could swallow it. He said, "You gonna make me do without water?"

Fargo unscrewed the cap from one of the canteens and held the vessel to his prisoner's mouth. Jessup greedily sucked down some of the water.

"How you think you're gonna stop Patch from gettin' those guns?" Jessup asked when he was through drinking. "There's a dozen of those boys and only one o' you."

"You don't think the citizens of Helldorado will help me?"

Jessup laughed. "Bates won't do anything without bein' paid for it. All Patch would have to do is offer him a share of the payoff, and Bates would cut your heart out and grin whilst he's doin' it."

"Bates isn't the only one in Helldorado."

Jessup spat. "Bunch o' damned sheep who're scared of their own shadows. No, Mr. Fargo, you ain't goin' to get any help from Helldorado."

"With Colonel Barrett's daughter missing, there must be search parties out looking for her," Fargo suggested. "If we run into one of those patrols, they'll be able to handle Donohue's bunch."

"If," Jessup repeated meaningfully. "That's just a matter of luck. You goin' to count on luck to save your bacon?"

"Whatever it takes," Fargo said.

They rode on. Fargo didn't replace the gag in Jessup's mouth after the old man promised not to complain. Jessup rode in sullen silence instead.

Fargo kept scanning the prairie, hoping to see a spiral of dust in the air or some other sign of a cavalry patrol. The rolling plains seemed to be empty, though.

Hours passed. The Ovaro moved easily in a ground-eating lope. Jessup's horse wasn't as strong, and as the afternoon wore on, Fargo had to hold down the stallion's pace to accommodate the other mount. When they had left the hideout, Donohue, Creed, and the rest of the gang had had less than an hour's lead on them. Fargo thought the gap had probably widened a little since then. But Donohue didn't plan to go into Helldorado to retrieve the rifles until after night fell, so Fargo was confident they could catch up to him.

Late in the day, when Fargo estimated that they were getting close to Helldorado, he spotted a haze in the air to the east. He reined in and brought Jessup's horse to a halt as well. To Fargo's experienced eyes, that haze could mean only one thing, and within minutes, it had coalesced into a cloud of dust being kicked up by a large group of approaching horses.

"Son of a bitch!" Jessup burst out. He knew what the dust in the air meant as well as Fargo did. "You're the luckiest bastard I ever did see!"

Fargo thought about all the punishment he had endured in the past week and didn't feel too lucky. But on the other hand, he was still alive after he'd been practically hip deep in the grave, so he supposed he couldn't complain about his luck. He watched the dust cloud long enough to have a good idea of the riders' course. Then he put the Ovaro into a trot again, moving forward to intercept the group of horsemen.

Of course, it was just possible that the riders were a Pawnee war party led by Cut Ear, he told himself with a grim smile, instead of a cavalry patrol. If that was the case, he and Jessup would have to run for their lives, and the odds would be against them. After riding part of the night and all day as they had, their horses were about played out, even the magnificent black-and-white stallion.

That luck Jessup had cursed was still with Fargo. As the riders came closer, he spotted their dark shapes at the base of the dust cloud. A few moments later, he could make out guidons flapping in the wind, and the blue of the troopers' uniforms. Fargo drew rein and waited for the soldiers to come to him.

He was a little surprised to see Colonel Barrett himself riding in the front of the group along with Lieutenant Ross. Barrett's face was more bleak and craggy than ever as he held up a hand to signal a halt. The patrol came to a stop about twenty yards from Fargo and Jessup, but Barrett and Ross came on ahead, halting when they were only a dozen feet away.

"Fargo!" the colonel exclaimed. "Where the hell have you been?"

"Trying to find those stolen rifles," Fargo replied coolly. "That *was* what you wanted me to do, wasn't it, Colonel?"

"I'm sorry," Barrett grated. "You see, my daughter is missing. You don't know her, but—"

"Actually, I do know her," Fargo cut in. Under the circumstances, he didn't want to delay revealing what he knew to Barrett. "She's safe, Colonel, at least for the moment. I know where she is."

Barrett's heels dug into the flanks of his mount and sent the animal forward. "Good Lord! Where is she, Fargo? Where is my daughter?"

There was no way to sugarcoat the news. "Patch Donohue has her," Fargo said. "Sergeant Creed is with him. He's one of Donohue's gang. They're holding Cass hostage so you won't interfere with them."

"Creed!" Lieutenant Ross said. "That . . . that filthy deserter! We've been looking for him, too. You say he . . . he's some sort of outlaw?"

"He's been in with Donohue, who stole the rifles, from the first," Fargo drawled. "That's one reason you couldn't find hide nor hair of the men who stole them, Lieutenant." Fargo left the other reasons unsaid—Ross's inexperience and sheer incompetence. The lieutenant was young. He might get over those failings if he lived long enough.

"My God!" Ross said in a wretched voice. "And those are the men who have Cassandra?"

"Pull yourself together, Lieutenant," Barrett snapped. "I'm as upset as you are, but right now we have to figure out a way to rescue her and get those guns back—if the outlaws still have them." He looked at Fargo.

"They do," Fargo confirmed. "The rifles are hidden in Helldorado. Donohue's bunch is on their way to get them now, so they can sell them to a Pawnee war chief named Cut Ear."

Barrett nodded. "I've heard of him. If he gets his hands on those weapons, there'll be a bloodbath out here on the plains, Fargo. We have to stop Donohue and Creed."

"But what about Cassandra?" Ross put in.

Barrett ignored him and gestured toward Jessup, who had sat there in gloomy silence throughout the conversation. "Who's this man? Why do you have him tied up?"

"Wait a minute," Ross said before Fargo could answer. "I think I know him. Doesn't he run the livery stable in Helldorado?"

"Among other things," Fargo said dryly. "His name's Hank Jessup. He's Donohue's uncle, and the one who's really been planning all the jobs Donohue has pulled around here."

"That's right," Jessup said. He uttered a vicious laugh. "I fooled all of you! And I'll fool you again if you don't watch out! You just wait and see if I don't!"

"He's out of his head," Ross muttered.

"Don't you believe it," Fargo said. "If I was you, Colonel, I'd assign a couple of those troopers to do nothing except keep an eye on Jessup and make sure he doesn't try some sort of trick."

Barrett nodded. "All right, Fargo, I'll take your word for it. Now, what are we going to do about Cass—and those guns?"

"We can't do anything that will put Cassandra's life in danger," Ross said quickly.

"The rifles are buried under what's left of Jessup's stable in Helldorado," Fargo said, ignoring the lieutenant. "The barn burned down a few days ago, but according to Jessup and Donohue, the crates with the rifles in them are buried deep enough so they should be all right. Donohue's going to get them tonight. If we ride into town right out in the open, we'll get a fight from Donohue's gang. But you've got enough men so that we should be able to handle them." Fargo paused. "The problem is, if we do that there's a good chance your daughter is going to wind up dead."

Barrett's face was stony and expressionless, but he couldn't hide the pain that flickered through his eyes. "We can't let them get the guns."

"Colonel!" Ross said. "You can't mean—"

Barrett turned on him savagely. "Lieutenant, I'll thank you not to say it! I know damned well what I mean. And I know what might happen. We . . ." His emotions caught up to him for a moment, and his voice broke a little. "We have to do our duty . . ."

"Hold on, Colonel," Fargo said. "There might be another way."

Barrett looked at him, and Fargo could see the eager hope bubbling up inside him. "Another way? How?"

"I said if we all rode into Helldorado, there would be a battle and Cass's life would be in danger. But if one man could slip into town and get her away from Donohue, then the rest of you could hit Donohue's bunch with everything you've got."

"One man?" Barrett repeated.

Fargo nodded. They both knew who that one man would be. The only one who would have a chance to pull off such a dangerous rescue.

"We're not far from Helldorado," Fargo said. "I'll leave as soon as it gets dark."

14

Keeping a tight rein on the impatience felt by Colonel Barrett and Lieutenant Ross was Fargo's main job as the sun sank toward the western horizon. At least Barrett, who was a seasoned officer, could fall back on his military experience, which had taught him that sometimes the best course of action was to do nothing until a more favorable time. Ross, on the other hand, was a young man in love, and as such he was operating almost entirely on instinct and emotion. Fargo had to convince him that Cass's best chance of coming out of this alive actually lay in waiting for nightfall.

"I want to go with you, Fargo," Ross announced as evening shadows finally began to gather.

Fargo shook his head. "That wouldn't be a good idea."

"Why not? Surely two men can sneak into Helldorado as easily as one."

Hank Jessup was sitting nearby on the ground, guarded by two troopers as Fargo had suggested. When he heard Ross's comment, he laughed merrily. "You just go right on thinkin' that, sonny. You talk Mr. Fargo into takin' you with him. I'll get a right smart bit of amusement out of it when Patch kills both of you."

Fargo ignored the old man. "I can move faster and quieter on my own," he told Ross. "I'm used to doing things like this, Lieutenant. You're not."

"I know," Ross said miserably. "I just . . ." He flailed his arms in the air in frustration, unable to find the words to express the fear and anger that were coursing through him.

"Snap out of it, Lieutenant," Barrett said. "You're not going to help Cass by getting so upset." The colonel took Fargo's arm and drew him to the side. "You talked to my daughter, Fargo. What in the world possessed her to do such a foolish thing as coming out here by herself?"

"You did, Colonel," Fargo said, putting it as bluntly as he knew how.

Barrett stared at him. "What the hell do you mean by that?"

"You decided to send her back East," Fargo said, "even though she didn't want to go."

Trenches appeared in Barrett's lean cheeks as the import of Fargo's words sunk in on him. "That's why Cass ran off?" he said in a half-whisper.

"She thought if she could find those guns, or even help me find them, that you'd see she could take care of herself and let her stay with you."

"My God." Barrett looked off into the dusk and then said again, "My God." He passed a hand over his face. "When Cass's mother . . . passed away . . . I thought it would be best for her if she were around another woman. I wrote to my sister, and she offered to take Cass in. I . . . I thought it would be best."

"It's not my place to say whether you were right or wrong, Colonel," Fargo said. "Hell, I haven't exchanged much more than a dozen words with your daughter. But that was enough to tell me that she's a pretty strong-willed young woman. Next time she says she doesn't want to do something, it might be a good idea to at least listen to her."

Barrett's features tightened with anger, then relaxed as he sighed. "You're right, Fargo. I don't have to like it, but by God, you're right."

"It didn't help matters, either, that Lieutenant Ross told her she was just a helpless female," Fargo said with a grin.

"He did?" Barrett looked like he didn't know whether to laugh or curse. "That young idiot. I'll have to have a talk with him. Not as his commanding officer, of course, but as Cass's father. Once we get back to Omaha, and everything's all right . . ."

The colonel's voice trailed away as he realized what a big assumption he was making. Fargo hoped they all got back to Omaha safely, but there was no way of knowing whether or not that would be the case.

He put a hand on Barrett's shoulder for a moment, then said, "It'll be full dark soon. I'd better get ready to pull out for Helldorado."

Fargo had plenty of ammunition for his guns, but he took some extra anyway from the supply carried by the patrol. He also borrowed a knife from one of the troopers and slipped it into the sheath that normally carried his Arkansas toothpick. On a mission such as the one facing him tonight, stealth was paramount, and that might mean killing silently. Cold steel was the best thing in the world for that.

Ross made one last try. "You're sure I can't go with you?"

Fargo shook his head and said, "Sorry, Lieutenant," even though he really wasn't. The odds against him were already high enough without him being saddled with an amateur.

Colonel Barrett extended his hand. "Good luck, Fargo," he said. "You'll signal us when you have Cass safely away from those outlaws?"

"Three fast shots together, a pause, then two more," Fargo said as he shook the officer's hand. "And when you come in, watch out for the townspeople. Most of them, like Bates, aren't innocent little lambs, but some of them are law-abiding citizens. I expect they'll keep their heads down when the shooting starts, though."

"We'll be as careful as we can," Barrett promised.

Fargo gave him a curt nod, then grasped the reins and the saddlehorn and swung up onto the Ovaro. With the slightest pressure of his heels, he sent the big stallion trotting off into the darkness.

Fargo kept an eye out for the lights of Helldorado. He didn't want to get too close before dismounting. He would have to make the final approach on foot. And yet he didn't want to leave the Ovaro too far from the edge of town, because he might need the horse in a hurry once he got his hands on Cass Barrett and spirited her away from Donohue's gang. A few minutes later, he spotted a scattering of telltale yellow glows up ahead and reined the stallion back to a walk. Those lights came from the windows of the buildings in the settlement.

Fargo rode a little closer before bringing the Ovaro to a halt. He dismounted and tied the reins to one of the small, scrubby clumps of brush that dotted the prairie. He left the Henry in the saddle sheath; any shooting he did tonight likely would be close work.

The moon wasn't up yet. Only the light from the stars filtered down from the darkened heavens. That was the way Fargo wanted it. He could see where he was going, but he would be more difficult to spot in the fainter light as he approached the town.

Where would Donohue, Creed, and the others be? he asked himself as he started forward on foot. The whole gang probably wouldn't go into town to retrieve the rifles. That would cause too much commotion, and Donohue wanted to keep things quiet so that he could use the hiding place again in the future if he needed to. A wagon would be required to haul away the crates of guns, and Fargo wondered where Donohue was going to get it. The outlaws could steal a wagon that was parked in town, Fargo supposed. Or it was possible that Donohue already had such a vehicle stashed somewhere? Would he wait until later in the night to go after the guns, when more of the inhabitants of Helldorado would be asleep? Or would he be too impatient for that?

Fargo had questions but no real answers. And all he could do, he told himself as he pondered the situation, was move ahead and deal with things as they came.

One thing he was certain of: Donohue and Creed would keep Cass Barrett close to them. She was their safe conduct out of Helldorado in case of trouble, and the two men wouldn't want her out of reach if they needed to use her as a hostage.

Fargo was only about a hundred yards from the most outlying of the buildings in town when he heard something behind him, something like the scuff of boot leather on the ground. He had been moving in a low crouch, using the clumps of brush for cover as much as possible, so it was fast and easy for him to go to ground. He dropped to a knee and twisted around, drawing the borrowed knife from the sheath on his calf as he did so.

A figure loomed out of the darkness, stumbling a little as it came toward him. Fargo's leg shot out, sweeping the man's legs from beneath him. Fargo's muscles reacted like steel springs—albeit rusty ones, due to all the beatings he had taken lately—as he pounced on the man who had been following him. Fargo's knee dug into the man's stomach, and his left hand clamped like a vise on the man's neck. Resting the tip of the knife against the man's throat just below the jawline, Fargo hissed, "Don't move!" When the man lay there unresisting, obviously with no intention of putting up a fight, Fargo loosened his hold a little on the man's throat and whispered, "Who are you?"

The reply was hoarse and half-strangled. "Lieu . . . Lieutenant Ross!"

Fargo bit back the angry curse that sprang to his lips. He wasn't surprised. Even as he'd been tackling the shadowy figure, he had suspected that it belonged to Ross. The shavetail simply hadn't been able to follow Fargo's orders and remain behind. Fargo suspected that Ross had slipped off without Colonel Barrett knowing anything about it. Barrett would have stopped him if Ross had told the colonel what he planned to do.

"Can . . . can you let me up now?" Ross croaked.

Fargo was tempted to refuse. In fact, he was tempted to reverse the knife, use the hilt to knock Ross unconscious, and leave the lieutenant there for the varmints to nibble on.

But then Ross would be liable to come to, stumble into Helldorado, and ruin everything. Nor did Fargo trust Ross to be able to get back to the patrol without giving away his—and their—presence. No, now that he was here, the best thing might be to keep him close, so that at least Fargo could keep an eye on him.

He just hoped that decision wouldn't wind up getting him killed.

"Shut up and listen," Fargo whispered with his lips pulled back from his teeth in a grimace. "You're getting your wish, Ross. You're coming into town with me. But you stay right with me, and you do exactly what I tell you to do, when I tell you to do it. You got that?"

Ross's head bobbed in a nod.

"Are you sure?" Fargo pressed.

"Yes. You're in charge, Fargo."

"Damn right." Fargo took the blade away from Ross's throat and let go of him. He pushed himself up off the lieutenant. He was about to sheath the knife when another sound made him stiffen. A horse had just blown out through its nostrils, maybe twenty yards away.

Fargo knew that Ross had made enough noise falling down that it could have been heard farther away than that. Which meant that if the horse had been over there when Fargo jumped Ross, the animal's owner probably had heard the commotion. And if the man was one of the outlaws, *that* meant he probably was sneaking up on them right now . . .

With that much warning, Fargo was already moving when he heard the sudden rush of footsteps coming toward him. He spun toward them and saw two men. Starlight glittered on the blade of a knife as it stabbed at him. He whipped his own knife around. Sparks flew and steel rang together as the blades met.

Fargo had been in many a knife fight. Even using an unfamiliar weapon instead of his Arkansas toothpick, he could hold his own against any one man. But there were two opponents here, and even as he parried the blow of the first man, the second one struck with the speed of a snake. Only Fargo's incredible reflexes saved him. He twisted out of the way just in time, so that the knife raked along his side rather than plunging into his body. The wound hurt like fire, but it was better than dying.

Since he was already twisting, he continued the movement,

bending at the waist and lashing out with his right foot. The heel of his boot drove into the belly of the first man, doubling him over and knocking him backward off his feet. Fargo dropped to the ground as the second man tried to gut him with the backswing from the thrust that had torn Fargo's side. The blade went over Fargo's head. He caught himself with his free hand and surged forward, striking out and up with the knife at the same time. The blade sliced deep into the second man's groin. He started to scream in agony, but the fingers of Fargo's left hand closed around his throat, choking off the cry. Fargo turned the knife and ripped upward with it, feeling the hot spill of blood across his hand. The man's body spasmed and then went limp. Fargo let go of his neck and let him fall to the ground.

That still left the first man to deal with. Fargo turned, expecting to have to fend off another attack immediately, but instead he saw a dark shape writhing on the ground. After a second, he realized that shape was actually two men struggling. One of them lifted an arm, then it came down and a blow landed with a crunching thud. The man who had been hit went still, while the other stood up shakily and turned toward Fargo.

"It's me. Lieutenant Ross."

Fargo nodded. Ross's pistol was in the lieutenant's hand. That was what Ross had used to hit the other man. From the sound it had made when it landed, Fargo knew the would-be killer had met his own end. Ross had crushed the man's skull.

"Well, we've cut down the odds by two, anyway," Fargo said.

"That man," Ross rasped. "I . . . I killed him—"

Fargo took hold of Ross's arm and pulled him down into a crouch. "That's right," Fargo told him in a half-whisper as he studied the prairie around them, alert for any sign that more of the outlaws were in the area. Not seeing or hearing anything suspicious, Fargo went on, "It's a damned good thing you did, too. They would have gutted us and never lost a second's sleep over it."

"But . . . but how do we know they were some of Donohue's men?"

"Who else would be out here right now?" Fargo asked. "And they came after us with knives, not guns. They didn't want to shoot any more than we did, because that would alert the folks in Helldorado that something's going on. Donohue and Creed don't want that. They want to slip in and out with those guns and nobody the wiser. That way they don't have to cut Bates in on the payoff."

Ross drew in a deep, ragged breath. "Well, if . . . if you're sure."

"Trust me, Lieutenant. You did the right thing. And you did it well."

That came as a little surprise to Fargo. Clearly, Ross could handle himself in a fight, at least as long as he was lucky. That was more than Fargo had expected from him.

"Let's go," he said. "There's only about a dozen of them now."

Ross swallowed hard. He was still shaky, but he managed to nod and say, "All right. I'm with you, Fargo."

With Fargo taking the lead, they left the dead men behind them and crept closer to the town. A moment later, Fargo spotted the horses he had heard. There were two of them, standing ground-hitched in a small depression. They had to belong to the two men who had attacked him and Ross, Fargo thought. But there weren't any others around.

That led to an intriguing thought. Donohue could have split up the gang and posted them in pairs around the settlement in an attempt to make sure that no one else got in or out of Helldorado tonight. With the Platte River forming the northern boundary of the town, no guards would be needed on that side. Donohue had a dozen men. That made six pairs . . . Fargo paused and did some figuring, trying to work out how far apart the teams of sentries would be. He decided that if he and Ross went straight past the spot where the two men had left their horses, there was a good chance they could reach the settlement without being observed.

If his theory was right.

Fargo grinned to himself. There was only one way to find out. He motioned Ross forward.

Eventually they were crawling forward on hands and knees and then slithering on their bellies as they neared the edge of town. The approach took a while. Getting in a hurry now could be deadly, Fargo knew. He paused frequently to look and listen, but neither saw nor heard anyone moving about. There were fewer lights burning in Helldorado now, too, as more of the town's citizens turned in for the night. Music played faintly, probably coming from Bates's saloon. That would be the only place in town still open for business this late.

Fargo swung to the east a little. That would allow him and Ross to come at the burned-down livery stable from the rear. He raised himself on his elbows and peered through the darkness, trying to sort out the buildings. He spotted the squat shape of Bert Abbott's blacksmith shop with the small cabin behind it. Next to the blacksmith shop was an indistinct smudge of blackness with what looked like twisted fingers sticking up out of it in places. That was the debris of the stable. A few studs from the walls were still standing.

There was movement in the darkness. Fargo strained his ears and heard a faint, chinking sound. Digging. Donohue and Creed were in the ruins of the stable at this very moment, digging up the stolen army rifles Donohue and Hank Jessup had hidden there.

Fargo looked for the wagon and finally spotted it, along with a team of horses standing next to the rubble. That was where Cass would be, he thought. Donohue and Creed would have trussed her up and gagged her and left her in the wagon.

Fargo touched Ross on the shoulder and then pointed without saying anything. He would have felt better about things if he could have sat the lieutenant down and explained to him in great detail everything they were about to do. But he would have to be satisfied with pointing and gesturing and hoping that Ross understood. Ross nodded to indicate that he did. Fargo hoped he was right.

Moving faster now because he had no way of knowing how close Donohue and Creed were to being finished with their chore, Fargo crawled toward the blacksmith shop. He and Ross would use Abbott's cabin and shop as cover to reach the street, and then make their way to the wagon. Once they made it to the vehicle, Fargo intended to grab Cass, hand her over to Ross, and tell them to get the hell away from there while he functioned as their rear guard. As soon as Cass was well clear, Fargo would fire the shots that would bring Colonel Barrett and the rest of the patrol on the double.

A dog started to bark as Fargo and Ross came even with the cabin where the blacksmith lived. Fargo motioned for Ross to get to his feet as he stood up and hurried forward. Speed was almost as important as stealth now. The barking might spook Donohue and Creed. On the other hand, dogs barked at anything and nothing, and the two outlaws might not be alarmed by the commotion. Other dogs began to bark elsewhere in town, taking up the canine hue and cry.

Fargo ran silently around the blacksmith shop and into the street. Ross followed close behind him, trying to be quiet, but not being so successful at it. Fargo angled toward the wagon, slowing down a little and motioning for Ross to do likewise. The Trailsman's keen eyes penetrated the darkness better than most, and he could see that none of the outlaws were standing guard over the wagon. Several yards beyond the vehicle, the burned-out ruins of the barn began. Fargo saw the two men working there, shovels biting into the dirt.

He dropped into a crouch as he reached the wagon. Ross came up beside him, struggling to control his breathing. The lieutenant was excited and scared and probably a little sick. He was also huffing and blowing so loud Fargo didn't see why they couldn't hear him all the way back in Omaha. Donohue and Creed didn't seem to notice, however. They were concentrating on their task, and the digging made enough noise that it covered up quieter sounds.

One of the diggers paused, though, and said in a voice

Fargo could barely make out, "What the hell are those dogs raisin' such a ruckus about?"

That was Creed, Fargo thought. He recognized the sullen rumble.

"Stupid dogs bark at anything," Donohue replied, echoing Fargo's thought of a few moments earlier. "Don't worry about it. Let's just get these crates up out of the ground."

"What if somebody comes out to take a look around?"

"Nobody's goin' to worry just because some mutt is yappin' its fool head off."

Fargo hoped Donohue was right about that. He didn't want anything disturbing the two renegades until he had Cass hustled off to safety.

He lifted his head to peer over the sideboards of the wagon. A shape was sprawled in the wagon bed, unmoving. Fargo had a bad few seconds when he thought that Cass might already be dead, but then he realized that she was just tied up and gagged, as he had expected. Her feet were lashed together tightly at the ankles, and her arms were pulled behind her back and her wrists tied. Fargo could even make out the bandanna that had been tied around her head and in her mouth as a gag.

Cass was lying facing away from him. He reached over the side of the wagon and laid a hand on her shoulder. She jerked in terror, and Fargo regretted that. But he rolled her toward him as fast as he could, leaned over so that his mouth would be closer to her ear, and hissed, "It's me, Fargo. Ross is with me. We're going to get you out of here."

Cass made a little whimpering sound of relief. Fargo stooped, pulled the knife from its sheath, and reached over the side of the wagon to cut the cords around her ankles first. As long as she could run, that was the most important thing right now. Her arms could be freed and the gag disposed of later.

The blade had just touched the ropes when Fargo heard a drumming of hoofbeats coming fast toward Helldorado.

His head jerked toward the sound. Who in blazes was

galloping in out of the night? One of Donohue's gang? It had to be. Colonel Barrett and the rest of the patrol wouldn't move in until he gave the signal.

But somebody was coming, sure enough, and Fargo knew that he had only seconds now to rescue Cass, fleeting instants of time that would be gone all too soon. He didn't want to cut her ankles, but he couldn't afford to be careful now. He sliced at the ropes holding her legs together.

Out in the ruined barn, Donohue heard the racing hoofbeats, too, and was startled into exclaiming, "What the hell!"

The ropes around Cass's ankles parted. Fargo barked at the lieutenant, "Grab her and get out of here!"

And at the south end of the street, the frantic rider galloped into town, waved his hat over his bald head, and shouted in a high-pitched, elderly voice, "Patch! Patch! The cavalry's comin! The cavalry's comin'!"

Hank Jessup had come back to Helldorado.

15

Fargo snatched his Colt out of its holster as Jessup veered the horse toward the burned-out livery stable. There was no need to keep quiet now. Fargo threw a shot at Jessup, not knowing if the old man was armed or not, but knowing he didn't want to risk his life, and the lives of Cass and Ross, on the question. Jessup kept coming, and whooping and hollering all the while, so Fargo knew he had missed.

And there wasn't time for another shot at Jessup, because Donohue and Creed had dropped the shovels, grabbed their guns, and were banging away at Fargo. Slugs thudded into the wagon beside him.

That wagon was empty now, because Lieutenant Ross had reached over the sideboards, grabbed Cass, and hauled her out, throwing her over his shoulder like a bag of flour. He broke into a stumbling run toward the blacksmith shop, which was the nearest shelter other than the wagon, and much more solid.

Fargo twisted, triggered twice toward the rubble, then broke the other way, heading in the opposite direction from Ross and Cass. He wanted to draw the outlaws' fire, and he succeeded. Bullets kicked up dust around his feet as he dashed toward the closest building, some sort of business that was closed down for the night. He threw two more shots toward Donohue and Creed, then flung himself forward in a dive that took him between the porch of the building and a water trough.

Fargo rolled onto his side and started reloading the

Colt. As he did so, he thought about what had happened and how everything had gone wrong. Jessup had escaped somehow from the cavalry patrol; that much was obvious. Fargo had warned Colonel Barrett that the old man was tricky. The fact that Jessup was here in Helldorado was proof of that.

Jessup knew that Donohue wanted to be discreet about recovering the stolen rifles. But he also knew that the gang wouldn't have a chance against the soldiers if the trap closed on them as Fargo planned. Better to reveal the hiding place than to lose the rifles entirely.

The rest of the gang would ride hell-for-leather into town when they heard the shooting. They had to be on their way already, Fargo thought. So would Barrett and the rest of the patrol. Even without Fargo's signal, the sounds of a pitched battle would draw the cavalry. More than likely the patrol was close by already, in pursuit of Jessup.

For now, the shooting had stopped. Shouts of alarm came from down the street as men poured out of Bates's saloon. Fargo ignored them. They weren't the threat; Donohue and Creed were. Fargo peered toward the ruined livery stable, but didn't see the two renegades anywhere. They had gone to ground, but probably they were trying to sneak up on him at this very moment.

He looked around. Jessup had vanished, too. There was no telling where the old man was. The only good thing Fargo could see was that Ross had reached the blacksmith shop with Cass. Assuming that Bert Abbott was the honest man he had seemed to be, he would help Ross protect Cass.

Fargo's pulse was hammering inside his head. He thought fleetingly of how nice it would be to spend a week at the King's Crown back in Omaha, making love with Nora Lazenby and playing cards and drinking in her brother's tavern. A week of nothing but taking it easy and recovering from everything that happened . . . He thought his restless nature could stand that.

A bullet hit the lip of the water trough a few inches above his head and ricocheted off, busting those pleasant thoughts all to hell and gone. Fargo saw the muzzle flash from the corner of the building in front of which he lay, and he snapped a shot toward it. At the same time, he heard feet thudding behind him.

Donohue and Creed had split up! That realization flashed through his mind. One of them had drawn his fire from the near corner of the building while the other had circled around behind it. Fargo surged up off the ground as a slug fired from behind him sizzled past his ear. He went over the water trough in a rolling dive as more bullets splashed into the muddy liquid. Fargo thumbed off two shots while he was in midair, firing first in one direction then the other. He didn't expect to hit anything, but he hoped to distract his enemies for a moment.

He landed hard on his shoulder, rolled over, and came up running. As he headed across the street toward another building, he saw men galloping into the southern end of the street. Those would be some of Donohuc's gang, he guessed. That was confirmed a second later when Donohue shouted, "It's Fargo! Get him!," and the newcomers started blazing away at him.

A wall of flying lead cut him off from the far side of the street. He stopped short and started to turn back the other way, but Donohue and Creed were both out in the open now, firing at him. There was nowhere for Fargo to go. He was truly between a rock and a hard place.

But then, with the blare of a bugle, the cavalry surged into Hclldorado right behind the rest of the outlaws. Guns blasted and men screamed and cursed, and in a matter of seconds, the south end of the street was a swirling, bloody melee between the soldiers and the members of Donohue's gang. Now that the owlhoots had their hands full, Fargo had a chance to shoot it out with Donohue and Creed.

Not alone, though. Lieutenant Jackson Ross burst out of the blacksmith shop with a pistol in his hand and shouted, "Sergeant Creed!"

The burly noncom was closer to the blacksmith shop than Donohue. Creed turned in that direction, firing smoothly and quickly as he pivoted, and Ross stumbled as the bullet ripped into him. His own gun smashed out two shots, though, and Creed was driven back into the wall of the building by the impact of the slugs. Creed got off another shot, but the bullet went into the dirt at his feet as Ross shot him a third time.

Meanwhile, Fargo and Donohue faced off. The street was lit up garishly by the muzzle flashes as each man fired twice. Fargo felt the wind of Donohue's bullets on his bearded cheek. Donohue stumbled, trying to close in on Fargo and fire again. Fargo beat him to it. The Trailsman's Colt roared, and Donohue's head jerked back as the bullet tore through the black eye patch, the empty socket behind it, and on through the outlaw's brain before bursting out the back of his head in a grisly shower of blood and bone fragments. Donohue was dead before his limp body smacked into the ground.

Fargo started reloading again as he trotted toward Ross, detouring just long enough to make sure Creed was dead. The front of the sergeant's uniform blouse was sodden with blood. There was no pulse in his neck when Fargo checked it. Fargo hurried on to Lieutenant Ross, who was leaning on a stump just outside the blacksmith shop. Cass Barrett was beside him, and her close-cropped fair hair shone, even in the darkness, as she fussed over him.

"Oh, my God, Jackson, you're wounded!" she cried out.

"I'm all right," he told her. "The bullet just nicked me."

"But there's blood all over your shirt!"

"I tell you, Cass, I'm fi—"

Then Ross fell over sideways, out cold. He would have hit the ground if Fargo had not been there to grab him and lower him more gently to the street.

Fargo straightened quickly, bringing up the freshly loaded Colt, as hoofbeats suddenly sounded close beside him. When he looked up, though, he saw Colonel Barrett reining in. Barrett practically threw himself off his horse and folded Cass into his arms as he hugged her like he intended to never let go.

"Cass, girl," Barrett said hoarsely. "Are you all right? Are you hurt? My God, if you are, I'll never forgive myself—"

"I'm fine, Pa, I really am. They didn't hurt me."

Barrett put his hands on her shoulders and looked down into her face. "Where are they?" he said. "Those bastards! I'll make them wish they'd never been born!"

Fargo said, "Creed and Donohue won't be wishing anything, Colonel. They're both dead."

Barrett nodded curtly, then looked down at Ross. "What about the lieutenant?"

"Let's take a look."

Fargo knelt beside Ross and opened his shirt as Bert Abbott approached from the blacksmith shop carrying a lantern. "You need some light, Mr. Fargo?" the smith asked.

"Thanks, Bert. Hold the lantern down here a little closer . . ."

Fargo was no doctor, but he'd had a lot of experience with gunshot wounds. After a quick examination of the bloody gash in Ross's side, he said, "He'll be all right. The wound's messy, but not serious. It just needs to be cleaned up and bandaged."

"I'll take care of that," Cass said without hesitation. "Pa, if you can get some of the troopers to carry him inside . . ."

Barrett turned to give the orders. Several of the cavalrymen who had ridden up and dismounted as Fargo was checking out the lieutenant's injuries sprang forward to obey.

"What about the rest of the gang?" Fargo asked Barrett as the troopers picked up Ross and carried him into the blacksmith shop.

"Dead, most of them, or wounded so badly that they soon will be. A few of them threw down their guns and surrendered. They'll meet their end on the gallows, for what they did to the men with that supply train."

Fargo nodded. Patch Donohue and his gang wouldn't be cutting a swath of murder and robbery through Nebraska Territory anymore, and Cut Ear and the Pawnee wouldn't spill innocent blood with those stolen guns.

"I reckon you'd like to have those rifles back now," Fargo suggested. He turned toward the burned-out livery stable. "They're over there."

Fargo and Barrett walked through the rubble. The smell of ashes was still strong, despite the passage of several days. They reached the spot where Donohue and Creed had been digging. It had been in one of the stalls when the stable was still standing, Fargo judged. Some straw spread over the ground would have concealed the digging that had gone on when the guns were buried there.

Now there was a good-sized hole. Barrett called more of his men over, and they used the shovels Donohue and Creed had dropped to finish enlarging it. Within minutes, the shovels thudded against the buried crates.

"Get them up out of there," Barrett ordered. His men bent to the task.

But a moment later, one of the troopers exclaimed, "Hey, Colonel, this box is mighty light to have rifles in it!"

Barrett leaned forward, and Fargo tensed. "What?" the colonel demanded. "Let's see."

The crate was lifted out of the hole. One of the soldiers used the butt of his pistol to knock off the lid. An empty crate gaped up at the stunned men surrounding it.

"Lose somethin'?"

Fargo turned in a hurry and saw that Mayor Ebeneezer Bates had sauntered out from the crowd of onlookers that had gathered once all the shooting was over. With a grim expression on his face, Fargo strode over to him.

"Bates, what do you know about this?"

"Me?" Bates asked innocently. "Why, I don't know nothin'. I just wondered if them army boys had lost somethin'. Some rifles, maybe."

"You know good and well what we're looking for," Fargo snapped. "Hell, you've probably known ever since I rode into Helldorado the first time!"

Bates tugged at his beard. "I could'a made a pretty good guess, I reckon. You see, there ain't much that goes on in this here town that I don't know about. I told you that from the first, Fargo. What I don't know is whether or not there might be a ree-ward for the safe return o' them guns."

Barrett came over to them in time to hear that comment. "By God, sir, if you know anything about those guns, it's your duty to tell us."

"It's a fella's duty to make a livin', too. I'm just sayin' that it seems fair there'd be a ree-ward—" Bates stopped short at the looks on the faces of Fargo and Barrett. He swallowed and said, "I dug 'em up. They're in the back room o' my saloon right now."

"When?" Fargo grated. "When did you dig them up?"

"A couple o' nights ago, after Hank Jessup dropped out of sight. Was he in on it, that old skunk? Was he workin' with Donohue?"

"He was Donohue's uncle," Fargo said. "And yes, he knew all about the guns. Donohue was going to sell them to the Pawnee. What were *you* planning on doing with them, Bates?"

"Why, I was gonna give 'em back to the army, o' course." Bates tried to sound as if his dignity had been mortally wounded. "I'm a law-abidin' citizen. Besides, if them guns had wound up in the hands o' Cut Ear and his savages, folks might've stopped headin' west on the Oregon Trail. Then where would I be? This here's the closest place a young feller with one o' them immigrant trains can find hisself a gal and a bottle of whiskey."

That made sense, Fargo thought. At least, it would to a money-grubbing rapscallion like Bates. But regardless of the mayor's motives, Bates had acted so that Donohue and Creed couldn't have reclaimed those guns even if Fargo and the cavalry hadn't showed up to stop them.

Bates jerked a thumb over his shoulder. "You can send some o' your soldier boys over to the saloon to fetch them guns, Colonel. Now, about that ree-ward . . ."

Something else Bates had said made Fargo think. He looked around and asked, "What happened to Jessup?"

He hadn't seen the old-timer since Jessup had galloped past shouting the warning to Donohue and Creed.

"If he knows what's good for him, he's still riding," Barrett said. "He got his hands on a knife somehow and wounded one of my men when he escaped. He'll hang, too, if we ever catch up to him."

Fargo thought about how slick Hank Jessup was, and he figured that somehow, the army would never see hide nor hair of that old man again. Of course, as wide as the trail ahead could be, it was plenty small when you least expected it. Fargo wouldn't be surprised if he crossed paths with the wily ol' bastard again, he just hoped he was on the right side of the smoking barrel when it happened.

The trail, wherever it led, certainly had its bag full of tricks in store. Fargo didn't know what he would find around the bend and behind the sunset, didn't care much either, as long as he kept moving on. Which was exactly what he aimed to do.

LOOKING FORWARD!

**The following is the opening
section of the next novel in the exciting
Trailsman series from Signet:**

THE TRAILSMAN #255
MONTANA MADMEN

*Bitterroot Valley, 1862—
There's gold in Devil's Creek,
and madness in the marshal.*

The trading post west of Fort Sheridan wasn't any different from a lot of those that Skye Fargo had seen—not much more than a ramshackle hut, dark and dirty, smoky and smelly, with a few tables and a makeshift bar. Anybody could turn up in a place like that, from the best to the worst, but it was usually the worst. The man should have known that, Fargo thought. He should never have brought the woman there.

But it was none of Fargo's business, or so he told himself. He had other things on his mind, but even so, his lake-blue eyes turned icy when he heard the comments of the men at the table in the darkest corner of the room.

There were three of them, and they wore heavy buffalo robes, though it was too far into the spring for such things. They smelled worse than the dead animals they'd taken the hides from, and their faces were hidden by heavy beards. Their voices were coarse and loud, as if they'd been drinking for quite a spell.

The couple could hear them, too, probably better than Fargo could. It was plain that they were trying to ignore the roughnecks, but Fargo figured that it would soon be impossible.

He was right. It wasn't long before one of the men stood up and said something that made the woman avert her face. The man and his friends laughed, and he walked over to the table where the woman sat, his heavy robe dragging on the hard-packed dirt floor. He wore a beaver hat that had seen better days. Some of the fur was missing, and what remained was stained and greasy.

The trading post owner, a short, skinny man named Barsett, was behind the rickety bar, and he started to reach for something that Fargo couldn't see, but one of the men still sitting at the table reached inside his robe and brought out a heavy Navy Colt and laid it on the tabletop with an audible thump. Barsett looked up, and the man shook his head at him. Barsett smiled a weaselly smile and walked to the far end of the room, where he pushed aside a dirty cloth that served as a curtain and went out. It was clear that he wasn't going to interfere with whatever happened.

The man with the pistol looked over at Fargo and gave him a gap-toothed grin as if to say that the fun was about to begin. The grin was not, however, an invitation for Fargo to join in. It was a clear sign that Fargo wasn't to do anything at all, other than to stay right where he was and ignore what was going on. Fargo took a drink of his sorry-tasting whiskey and didn't say a word.

The big man had reached the woman's table by then, and he was looking down at the man Fargo assumed was her husband, who started to stand up.

"Don't, Moses," the woman said, but she was too late because Moses was already halfway out of his chair.

The big man put out a ham-sized hand and shoved Moses back into the chair so hard that it wobbled backward and nearly overturned.

"You just be quiet and keep your seat, Moses," the big man said, "while I talk to this pretty little lady here."

She was pretty, all right, Fargo thought, or at least what he could see of her was. She had night-black hair and delicate features, with a wide mouth and big black eyes. She was wearing a heavy man's shirt that effectively covered any other charms she might have above the waist, and her lower body was hidden by the table where she sat.

She looked up at the man and said, "Leave us alone. Please. Just go away."

He grinned down at her and said, "You can call me Tom, and I ain't goin' away. I like the way you say please. I think I'd like to hear you say it again."

"Please," she said, looking down at the table.

The big man looked around at his friends and said, "Ain't that just about the sweetest thing you ever heard?"

He laughed, and one of them said, "It sure is, Tom. Tell her to say it one more time."

"You heard him," Tom told her. "Say it again."

The woman, who was still looking down at the table, opened her mouth, but this time no sound came out.

"Say it," Tom told her, his voice rough with anger.

"Leave her alone," Moses said.

"No, Moses," his wife said, but again she was too late. Moses was already clawing awkwardly for the pistol he wore at his side.

Tom didn't give him a chance to get it. He grabbed Moses by the collar and jerked him out of the chair.

"Don't ever try to pull a gun on me, son," Tom said. He threw Moses to the floor and nodded toward the table in the corner. The man who had laid the pistol on the table picked it up and fired twice. The first bullet struck Moses in the center of the chest. He was probably already dead when the second bullet took off the side of his jaw.

The sound of the shots echoed in the room, and for a while all Fargo could hear was the ringing in his ears. He smelled the bitter powder smoke and wondered again what a man like Moses had been doing in the trading post and why he'd brought the woman there.

Tom was saying something to the woman, but he kept his voice low, and Fargo couldn't quite hear what it was. The woman probably couldn't either, as she stared in shocked silence at the dead man, her eyes wide in disbelief.

The two men at the other table were laughing. Fargo couldn't hear them, either, but he saw their wide mouths and squinted eyes as the shooter dropped his Colt back on the table.

Fargo looked back at the woman. She eased out of the chair and onto the floor as if she wanted to cradle the dead man's head in her arms but was too sickened by the blood and tissue to do it.

Tom reached for her, but she struck away his hand. She was spirited, and that seemed to make him angry. He reached again, grabbing a fistful of her shirt. She tried to pull away, but he drew her up from the floor and to him. When he had her standing, he opened the buffalo robe with one hand and hugged her against his chest with the other. He pressed his bearded face to hers for a kiss. She turned her head aside, but that didn't bother Tom. He nuzzled her neck like a horse eating oats while she struggled to break his grip.

Fargo told himself that it wasn't his problem. He had things to do, and he couldn't let himself be distracted by the troubles of other people. They should have known better than to get themselves in such a bad fix, and if they had blundered into a bad situation, well, they deserved what had happened. Besides, Fargo had learned the hard way that nearly every time he got mixed into somebody else's business, it led to trouble for him. And he didn't need any more trouble right at the moment.

He told himself all that, but it wasn't helping much. He could see the two men laughing at their table, licking their lips in anticipation of what was to come. Fargo had a good idea of what that would be. As soon as Tom had his way with the woman, he'd give her to them, and by the time they were done with her, there wouldn't be much more left of her than there was of those buffalo the men had skinned for their robes.

Fargo sighed. He couldn't see himself letting that happen, even though he was sure he'd regret stepping in. He stood up and faced the men at the table. He was so quick that they hadn't even stopped laughing before his Colt was in his hand. The one whose pistol was on the table made a grab for it, but Fargo put a bullet in the bridge of his nose before he could get it clear of the tabletop.

The other man threw open his robe and pulled his own gun. Fargo let him get it almost level before he shot him in the right eye.

Fargo then whirled around to see that Tom had thrown the woman aside. She had landed on the table, knocking it over, and it had fallen on top of her after she hit the dirt floor.

Tom had his pistol out, and he was smiling at Fargo. "You shouldn't have done that, friend."

"I'm not your friend," Fargo said.

"No, I guess you ain't," Tom said.

He was about to pull the trigger when Fargo shot him the first time. Dust puffed out of the robe where the bullet struck, and Tom looked surprised. He looked even more surprised when Fargo shot him again, the bullet striking him in almost the same place the first one had. He slumped to his knees on the floor, looking up at Fargo, his eyes stunned. His beaver had fallen off and rolled to the side.

"You son of a bitch," he said.

Fargo didn't bother to answer. He just waited. He didn't have to wait long.

Tom fell forward on his face. His left leg twitched once, and the toe of his boot kicked the dirt floor. Then he was still.

The room was full of acrid smoke. Now that the shooting was over, Fargo waved it away from his face. Then he went back to his table and had a drink from his whiskey glass.

The woman stirred and looked around, wide-eyed. Fargo put the whiskey glass down on the table. He went over to the woman and helped her to her feet. What with all the shooting in the enclosed space, it would be a while before either of them could hear much of anything, so he led her outside and leaned her against the wall. Her shoulders shook as sobs racked her body, and Fargo left her to her grief.

It was a warm spring day. There wasn't a cloud to be seen in the high blue sky, and the grass around the trading post waved in the breeze. Fargo stood and let the sun warm him.

After ten or fifteen minutes, he started hearing sounds again, mainly the sobs of the woman. He was surprised she hadn't stopped crying by now.

He left her where she was and went back inside. The weasel-faced Barsett was standing over Tom's body, looking like he was about to cry, too. He wasn't grieving, however. He was just angry.

Barsett turned to Fargo and said, "You son of a bitch. What are you gonna do about all this?"

"Not one damn thing," Fargo told him. "This is your fault, Barsett. If you'd pulled your shotgun out from under the bar before it started, it never would've happened."

"Goddammit, I'll set the law on you."

"The hell you will. You know what they'd have done

to that woman. You probably would've helped, you little bastard."

Barsett opened his mouth, then looked at the face of the big man in the buckskins and closed it.

"That's better," Fargo told him after a few seconds of silence. "What you'd better do is bury those three and forget about anything ever happening here. It won't be the first time."

Barsett didn't deny the accusation. Finally he said, "Who's gonna pay me for the damages?"

"I don't see any damages," Fargo said. "Just four dead men. You can keep the robes off those three, and you can take whatever else they have on them for your trouble."

Barsett thought it over. It didn't matter to Fargo what the man decided. Fargo was leaving, no matter what.

"I guess that's fair," Barsett finally said. He seemed about to say something else, but he caught himself and clamped his mouth shut.

"I know what you're thinking," Fargo said. "You can have their horses, too. I don't care."

Barsett rubbed his hands together in satisfaction.

"What about the other fella?" he asked.

"His things go with the woman."

"Yeah, I figured. What about her?"

"You can't have her," Fargo said.

"A man like you don't need a woman taggin' along with him. What're you gonna do with her?"

It was a good question, and Fargo hadn't really thought that far ahead. He said, "We'll have to see about that."

He left Barsett standing there and went outside. The woman was still right where he'd left her, but she'd stopped crying. Fargo looked at her appraisingly.

"They killed Moses," she said, meeting his gaze.

"They did that," Fargo agreed. "He should've known better than to bring a woman like you out here with nobody to back him up. You should've been with a party, or had a guide."

Fargo had taken people all over the West. He knew about guides, and he knew about all the dangers that people could encounter, from Indians to animals to weather. And men like Tom and his partners.

"We couldn't afford a guide," the woman said.

Fargo looked back at the door of the trading post as if he could see what was inside it.

"I know what you're thinking," the woman said. "If we'd spent the money, Moses would be alive by now. But we didn't have the money to spend even if we'd wanted to. That's why we were going west. My brother's there. He says there's gold. Moses was going to try his luck."

Fargo looked the woman over. He'd been right about her looks, and now that he could see more of her, he knew that her body lived up to the promise of her face. She was wearing denim pants that fit tightly around her well-rounded rump, and her legs were long and slim.

"Where were you headed?" he asked.

"Devil's Creek. Did you ever hear of it?"

"I've heard of it," Fargo said.

"I'll never get there now. My God. What am I going to do?"

"I can take you there," Fargo told her.

"What?" She looked at him quizzically. "Why would you do that?"

"Because," Fargo said, "I'm headed there myself."

No other series has this much historical action!

THE TRAILSMAN

To order call: 1-800-788-6262

SIGNET HISTORICAL FICTION   (0451)

Ralph Cotton

"Gun-smoked, blood-stained, gritty believabilty...
Ralph Cotton writes the sort of story we all hope
to find within us."—Terry Johnston

"Authentic Old West detail."—*Wild West Magazine*

HANGMAN'S CHOICE   20143-4
They gunned down his father in cold blood. They are his
most elusive enemies, the outlaws known as *Los Pistoleros*,
and they're still at large. But Federal Deputy Hart will not
give up...

MISERY EXPRESS   19999-5
Ranger Sam Burrack is once again driving the jailwagon
filled with a motley cargo of deadly outlaws, whose
buddies are plotting to set them free. But with the Ranger
driving, they're in for quite a ride.

Also available:

BADLANDS	19495-0
BORDER DOGS	19815-8
JUSTICE	19496-9
BLOOD ROCK	20256-2

To order call: 1-800-788-6262

S525